WHY THE VAMPIRES DON'T NEED US

V. P. NIGHTSHADE

SOHMER PUBLISHING

CONTENTS

COPYRIGHT

ISBNs: EPUB: 978-1-960139-21-4 | PBK: 978-1-960139-22-1
First edition

THE VAMPIRIS BLOODLINE SERIES

READING ORDER

A Twisted Fairy Tale Obsession

V. P. Nightshade

Steamy Fairy Tale Retellings

STEP INTO THE ENCHANTING world of A Twisted Fairy Tale Obsession, where our reimagined timeless fairy tales have a spell-binding, mesmerizing, steamy twist, offering readers a fresh adult perspective on beloved stories they thought they knew. Each installment in this captivating series transports readers to fantastical realms where love, sacrifice, and destiny intertwine in unexpected ways. From the ethereal forests of Beauty's Beast to the mystical depths of the Mer Kingdom, prepare to embark on an unforgettable journey through the interconnected threads of each narrative, where revelations linger like the echoes of a fairy tale's magic.

With each turn of the page, prepare to be swept away by the allure of these reimagined fairy tales, where love defies boundaries, sacrifices shape destinies, and the echoes of magic linger long in your heart after the last chapter ends. Embark on a journey unlike any other, where each enchanting tale weaves the essence of love, magic, and a steamy twist into its very fabric.

STEAMY ALIEN ROMANCE

V. P. NIGHTSHADE

Extraterrestrial Desires:

The Cicadian Commanders
An Alien Science Fiction Romance Series

We Want Your Women...And Your World!

DEEP BENEATH THE ARID deserts lies an ancient secret - a dormant alien spaceship that has awakened after 17,000 years. General Zorax and his elite Commanders emerge from their stasis pods to fulfill their audacious mission: conquer Earth to preserve their dying race. However, they soon discover that modern humanity is not as easily conquered as anticipated. Armed with advanced technology and cloaking capabilities, the Cicadian warriors blend seamlessly among humans while searching for traces of their lost civilization.

As General Zorax leads his Commanders across the nation, they encounter Earth women who stir deep desires within them. Duty compels them to take mates from these modern females, further complicating an already perilous situation. Passion ignites between species, testing loyalty and challenging the boundaries of love. Can General Zorax and his warriors fulfill their mission while navigating the intoxicating allure of Earth women?

Pick up an alien for yourself today!

The General's Awakening: A Scifi Alien Romance Invasion, Book 1

NAKED REVENGE

A DISH BEST SERVED COLD

NEMESIS, THE IMMORTAL GODDESS of Vengeance, is running out of time. Summoned by her divine parents to leave Earth forever, she must fulfill one last mission: bringing justice to nine betrayed women while securing a future for her nine shapeshifting monster sons.

Disguised as Miss Neme, a mysterious coffee shop owner, she listens to her patrons' stories of heartbreak and betrayal. Each woman's pain becomes a quest for justice, aided by one of Nemesis's sons—creatures like the Minotaur, Sphinx, and Hellhound. But these monsters have a deeper purpose: to find true love and forge bonds that will ensure their survival in the mortal world after Nemesis is gone.

This series blends mythology, romance, and revenge into nine gripping stories where love ignites in the most unexpected places, danger lurks in every shadow, and justice is served with fiery passion. As Nemesis races against time, she fights not only for these women but also for her sons, hoping to leave behind a legacy of love, strength, and redemption.

Prepare for a journey of STEAMY passion, vengeance, and unbreakable bonds in "Naked Revenge: A Dish Best Served Cold," a thrilling saga of myth and modernity where the

power of love collides with the need for justice.
https://mybook.to/NakedRevenge

A Note to the Reader
Combat Book Pirates

A BIG THANK YOU!

To My Readers ~

Who are looking for something with a little more bite~

I look forward to reading your reviews and comments!

To My Sons ~

The Things Mom's do for their kids!

As always, to that Grumpy Man ~

I'm glad you are still paying my bills!

I love you, baby!

EPIGRAPH

WHY THE VAMPIRES DON'T NEED US

They drank the blood of sacred flesh,
To steal the light and bind it fresh.
From cross to crown their thrones were made,
On lies and ash, on love betrayed.

But truth still burns with holy fire,
In rebels' hearts, in funeral pyres.
And one who bore the world's lament,
Became the blade their empire sent.

So whisper not of fate or kings—
A mother's scream can shatter wings
The dead may rise, the dark may reign
But blood remembers love and pain.

Her pen became a sharpened stake,
Each word a wound no fiend could fake.
She wrote in flame, in flesh, in bone,
To curse the tyrant on his throne.

The sun once scorned now crowned her brow,
Though cursed with fangs, she made a vow:

If death would keep her sons alive,
She'd burn to ash and never rise.

Yet rise she did—reborn, defiled,
By monster's touch and devil's guile.
But still her name on every breath—
Sage Steel, the fire that danced with death.

~ V. P. Nightshade
Read By The Author

My YouTube Channel:
https://www.youtube.com/@v.p.nightshade

Notes from the Author
Why The Vampires Don't Need Us

THANK YOU FOR TAKING the time to read my book! If you have read any of my previous works, (and if you haven't, you SHOULD) you know that I am known for mixing genres – but they always have romance involved.

Warning:
This story is not a romance!
Nor was it ever intended to be.

I wrote the original draft of this story in 2010, but I never took the time to clean it up, edit it, and publish it. In 2024, we brushed it off and ripped it apart and put it in a toned-down episodic format to submit to Amazon's Velly's Contest. When Amazon did away with the Vella format, we decided to republish it in its novel format and make a ton of improvements. With the help of some dedicated people, I have got that done now. We have ramped up the horror with this one! It hits you right in the gut. And I think it is one of the best books that I have ever published.

I hope you enjoy it! Please don't forget to follow me on Amazon and leave comments, ratings, and reviews after you have read the story. Your thoughts are so appreciated!

~ *V. P. Nightshade*

REBEL ADVISORY

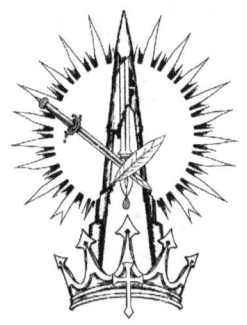

THIS FILE IS PART of the encrypted archive titled *Why The Vampires Don't Need Us*, distributed by known insurgents and forbidden by Crimson Empire Decree §418.7.

The following material contains content deemed psychologically destabilizing by the Vampire Authority. Proceed only if prepared for the full, unredacted truth.

This document includes:

- **Explicit bloodshed and brutal violence**
  (torture, executions, rebellion warfare, and vampire combat)

- **Body horror and graphic transformations**
  (burning, mutation, resurrection, and decay)

- **Psychological warfare and manipulation**
  (coercion, obsession, and state-sanctioned gaslighting)

- **Blasphemous accounts of divine betrayal**
  (including the desecration of sacred figures and theology)

- **Captivity and martyrdom**
  (voluntary self-immolation, sacrifice for the resistance)

- **Themes of parental loss, loyalty, and unbearable choice**

- **Mentions of self-inflicted death and violent retribution**

- **Insurgent propaganda**
  (calls for rebellion, uprising, and the extermination of tyrants)

- **Emotional trauma, existential dread, and moral corruption**

If you've known grief, lived in shadow, or bled for freedom — this story is for you.

If you're not ready to face the fire, close this file and walk away.

If you are...
Welcome to the Resistance.

"Words are blood. Blood is truth." — *The Wraith*

THE FALL OF THE WRAITH

Wraith? You there?

Hey, Fang-hater! Yes, I'm here. I'm glad to reconnect and that you are still kicking around out there! It's been a while. Nice to see that the dark web still has its uses.

What have you been up to?

Me? Not much, really. I have had a lot of alone time, recently. A lot of time to think. Too much. Hey, can I ask you something?

Always. Anything.

Anything? Well, I wouldn't ask just anything.
That could get rude! :)
Just something real specific.

Have you ever really screwed something up? I
mean fucked it up so badly that it is absolutely
beyond repair, recovery, or redemption?

No matter what you sacrifice, money or blood,
nothing will ever make up for it.

...

No.

No? Well, lucky you, because I have.

I have completely botched things up. The entire world. And I don't even think my dying
will help the situation; in fact, it might make it
worse.

I don't know what you mean.

That's because you have never screwed something up so goddamn bad that you wanted to
die, but know that even more horrible things
would happen if you did.

Did you mean to do it?

What? Of course, I didn't mean to do it! I don't think anybody would.

I didn't even know that I was causing any harm. Not that it makes a difference, I guess.

You know something; I believe the biggest fuckups come from people who truly have no inkling how much lasting damage they are truly causing, because they think they are doing something good.

For instance?

For instance? I will give you two. George Bush, 43, not 41, and Gorbachev bringing down the wall are two great examples. 'Good intentions' and all of that nonsense.

I don't see the connection.

It's the lack of critical thinking. You know being able to see three or more steps beyond any action.

???

Gorbachev. Three points: 'loose nukes', making the Russian Mafia a force to be reckoned with, and covert 'evil' instead of overt 'evil'.

And Bush?

Bush? That's too easy.
The. Iraq. War.

Enough said.

They did things that they thought were going to be good. But ended up fucking up other shit!

My point is, that I didn't mean to royally fuck up, either!
Hell, I was just doing my job! I was entertaining people; you know, giving them a mental outlet. It is just a job, after all! I was just trying to make a living.

You know in all the times that we have talked over the years, you've never told me what you used to do…you know, in the BEFORE.

Oh, I am sorry; I didn't tell you, did I?
Me, I write.

Really??? That's interesting!

Hey, don't get excited. lol I'm just a simple writer. Novels, mostly. I never aspired to War and Peace. And I am no Stephen King or J. K. Rowling, either. I just write teen-adult horror fiction.

What's that entail?

Well. Basically, I come up with an idea for a scary story and flesh it out with some misunderstood, sexy, brooding guy as the hero and some young naïve hottie looking for her first kiss. And hey, you have a story.

Did you make a lot of money?

It sold okay. I made a living at it. Heck, there was a staggering 110,000 of us actively writing in the genre. So you could say it was … competitive. Most people didn't get rich doing it, and your fan base was pretty fly-by-night.

I mean, they are not just reading you, but everybody who writes like you, and a person can only afford so many books. So...

Did you like it?

Yeah, I did.

I liked to write it and to tell you a secret ... I even liked to read it.

I know, putting money in the competition's pockets; but hey, even I needed some mental relaxation from the daily grind every once in a while.

The appealing thing about reading it was that it was an easy read, not too scary, kind of romantic and, most importantly — fiction.

Or so I thought.

The truth was so much more fantastic than even my creative mind could have come up with — fantastic, horrific, and fatal.

For everybody.

What made you want to be a writer?

Writing is kind of a singular activity, you know. I have a solid command of the English language, but I think one of the main reasons I pursued it as a career was that I was never skilled at dealing with people. Not directly, anyway.

Not face-to-face.

So, you were always a writer, then?

No, but I was kind of pushed that way.

When I interacted with people either in normal 9-5 jobs or social situations, I was always amazed by some of the things that people would do when they interacted with each other that were cruel, self-centered, often ridiculous, and downright stupid – with a capital STUPID.

Experiencing it firsthand and then coming home to watch and listen to these interactions on the evening news, talk television, radio, and 'reality' shows made me hate the whole concept of public education and a society that would tolerate such idiotic behavior.

There was no politeness in speech, no manners in personal actions; heck, no sense of responsibility in any actions taken at all! No rational thoughts, no follow-through.

The killer thing to me was that it was either tolerated or ignored.

And in certain regions of the country, rude and crude were wholeheartedly embraced as a valid form of communication.

It just used to shock the hell out of me!

It's different now.

Yeah.

Now, with all the Changes that have happened over the past few years, I actually find that I miss it.

I miss the humanity. I miss people. Even those who were rude and stupid.

I would give almost anything to see the type of rudeness and stupidity that used to rule the day.

That's better than the fear and loneliness.

You are not alone right now.

You have me.

We have this.

True. Even after all the death and bloodshed that the world has endured during the Change, we still have the Internet.

What a wonderful invention that turned out to be!

So wonderful even They use it to talk to each other – to Their friends.

It's the way that You and I talk to each other.

Except we are on the dark web without all the bells and whistles.

And They are not.

Fang-hater? You are my friend, aren't you?

Of course I am, Wraith. I have been for many years.

I'm glad. I think of you as my friend, even though we have never met.

Which, if you think about it, is probably a good thing, since gathering in any numbers can be fatal now. But we humans need it, this communication.

Especially between you and me; humans have to be able to communicate.

It's not life without communication, is it?

No. People were not meant to be alone.

I think communication, even though not face-to-face, nor audible, must be some sort of requirement in order to avoid going crazy.

At least avoiding the insanity of just trying to survive another night; hiding in the dark.

True.

It's good to know that someone else is out there, someone we can talk to, someone who understands us.

Someone who shares our concerns, our fears, our hopes.

Someone we can trust.

Someone who doesn't want to murder us.

Yes. It's good to have a friend. Even if it is only through the internet.

Sometimes I worry about my internet friends, especially when they don't talk to me for a while. I wonder if they are okay, if they are safe. And then, just when I think they are gone, I hear from them.

Sometimes it's just a couple of lines, to say, 'hi I am still here', 'moved to a safer location', 'lost electricity for a few days', or 'just barely escaped the goons'.

You know all the silly reasons that you get from your Internet friends when they aren't online for a while.

Yes.

I know this might seem irrational ...

???

When I hear from them, I feel relieved; then I get mad at them, cause don't they know how worried I was?

Don't they care I was worried? Don't they know they are important to me?

Am I not important to them?

You could always 'un-friend' them if they cause you such distress.

No. I could never 'un-friend' them, even if they don't care about me as much as I care about them.

Not now, they are all that I have that keeps me here ... grounded ... human.

In the end, after all, a disappointing friend is far better than a deadly enemy. Right?

True.

But that doesn't apply to you and me, does it?

No. Never. We are good friends.

True

...

You never said. What did you do? How did you screw up?

Wraith? Are you still there?

Sorry, I got sidetracked.
My mind ... has been ... all over the place ... recently.

Perhaps deep down, I truly didn't want to think about it.

But, it's funny really. Sort of. The answer, I mean. Not what happened.

Never what happened.

The answer is:
I was good at my job.

I don't get it.

How would that be a screw up?

It's simple. I was good at my job, but I didn't believe.

I didn't believe in Them.

You see, my writing made it seem like I was a believer; even when I didn't believe at all.

Everyone who read my books thought I believed. They were reading my books too, and soon They too came to believe.

I don't...

Listen! I was good at my job ... and everyone has paid for it. My writing and my stories, my silly stories which were full of happy endings, acceptance, and admiration for the strange and wonderful.

They used my writing and my stories. My ideas ... gave Them ideas.

Gave ... Him ... ideas.

My stories made Them dream; dream of conquest; dream of a world that could be Theirs for the taking.

My stories helped make Them acceptable to everyone; at least by most people. It was something that They counted on.

Relied on it, in fact.

That acceptance ... made possible through my stories over the years. It was something They used.

They molded themselves to what I had written, molded Their behaviors, put forth Their best face ...

Their most beautiful face.

Wraith...

> My stories made people believe They were be-nign, stricken, even friendly and loving, and most importantly, for Their success ... safe.

Wraith...

> My words made Them seem wonderful and magical ... and tame-able through our love.

Wraith...

> My stories helped Them create secret plans, while They pretended to build a society that could thrive amongst us, work beside us, and then ... They brought us to our knees.

Wraith!

> My words led them to action.

> My words led them to success.

Wraith!

> And IT'S ALL MY FAULT!

WRAITH!!!

I press my palms flat against the cold stone floor of my cell, feeling each uneven surface and gritty texture. My fingers brush the laptop sitting across my legs as I sit crisscross applesauce and lean my back against the stone wall. This laptop, one of the few pleasures I am allowed, is a lifeline in this tomb of despair that is the Washington National Cathedral. The screen's glow is the only light here, casting shadows that dance upon the walls like goblins at a macabre ball.

I draw a shuddering breath, the air heavy with the stench of iron and fear, and continue to type.

"Once," I whisper to myself as much as to the unseen ally awaiting my words, "vampires were fantasy. Creatures of the night bound by the pages of my novels."

Each keystroke echoes in my heart — my burial hymn for the world that used to be. A world where my books, with their seductive and brooding vampires, ignited imaginations rather than kindled a nightmare. How naïve we all were, believing in the separation of fiction and reality, until reality bared its fangs.

"Romance turned to horror," I continue, typing out the confession that burns inside me. "The seed planted by my stories blossomed into trust, and from that trust—their empire rose."

My mind shifts, flitting through memories like pages torn from a diary. The Blue Ridge Mountains loom in my recollection, painted in shades of rebellion and resilience. Here, in the silent bastion of our resistance, my sons and I became more than authors and readers; we became warriors. "The Wraith" they called me, a name whispered in reverence by some, in hatred by others.

"Tommy, Danny," I murmur, their names a talisman against the darkness. We planned under the cloak of night, using the very myths I penned to orchestrate our defiance. Guerrilla tactics, covert strikes—our every move a calculated risk to push back the crimson tide that threatened to drown humanity.

"Mother by day, leader by night." The duality of my existence is a jagged edge upon which I balance, bleeding yet unbroken. The weight of my secret, the cost of my two lives—it's a burden I carry alone. With the cathedral's grandeur now a mockery of hope, I cling to the desperation that fuels my fight.

And I type, racing against time, against discovery, against the encroaching darkness that seeks to snuff out the last embers of resistance. My last message of the night is a coded beacon, a flare sent into the void.

I hope it finds those still standing in the shadows.

"Until tomorrow," I sign off, the familiar prickling of anxiety at the back of my neck a reminder that any word could be my last. Silence falls like a shroud over me, and I close the laptop, surrendering once again to the oppressive embrace of the waiting dark.

The abrupt rhythm of Victor's footfalls beat a somber lament upon the cathedral's stone floor, each echo a stark reminder of the precarity of my existence. I freeze in place, listening intently as the sounds fade before I dare to breathe again.

I have become something akin to a phantom in these hallowed halls, an apparition, rarely seen, weaving stories not of fantasy, but of coded rebellion. Each narrative I craft for the vampires doubles as a cryptic missive to those who remain unyielded, who look to "The Wraith" for guidance from the shadows. My words are their weapons, my sentences their stratagems.

Under my fingers, the laptop keys click with frantic urgency, a speedy but disjointed symphony that punctuates the silence. It is a race against time and detection, a delicate dance with fate as I embed secret instructions within the fabric of my prose, hoping they will slip unnoticed past vigilant eyes. The vampires are convinced they have extinguished the human spirit, but it remains vibrant, throbbing in the subtext of every paragraph I write.

Yet, with each message sent, the noose tightens. Paranoia is a constant companion, whispering of betrayal with every creak of the ancient wood, every flicker of shadow across the cold, damp walls of my cell. My hands tremble, betraying the fear I must never show to the enemy.

Never ... show.

A shiver runs down my spine as I cast my mind back to the day Praetor Pilatus stood before me, his presence an embodiment of the power that had ripped me from my sanctuary and placed me into a prison. His icy blue eyes had locked onto mine, his gaze piercing through my defenses as if he could see the very core of my being.

"Your words have moved many," he had said, his voice silk over steel, a veneer of admiration that failed to mask the threat beneath. "Now, you shall write them for us."

His request—or rather, his command—was a sacrilege to my soul: to write a false history glorifying these monsters, to turn my gift into a tool for their propaganda. I remember how the air seemed to grow thin, the weight of his expectation squeezing the breath from my lungs. In that moment, his unnerving calm scrutinized me and exposed the true horror of my captivity.

"History is written by the victors," Pilatus continued, the corners of his mouth tilting up in a semblance of a smile. The chill in the room grew palpable, the darkness encroaching ever closer, as if to listen.

"Indeed, it is," I replied, my voice steady despite the tempest raging within. "And yet, history also has a way of revealing the truth in time."

His smile vanished as quickly as it had appeared, replaced by a hardening of his features that spoke volumes more than any threat could convey. In that silent exchange, the battle lines were drawn—not of swords and blood, but of wills and wits.

"Consider it your magnum opus," Pilatus had said before turning on his heel and departing, leaving me alone with the crushing realization of the task set before me.

I knew my choices: write or die.

Still, I knew who I was. I was Sage Steel. Though ensnared, I was not yet broken. With a defiant spark, I prepared for the morrow, knowing that in the war of shadows, it is the pen that can be mightier than the sword.

Or in this case, *fang.*

So I waited, the air in my cell as silent as Victor, my personal praetorian. And I strategically planned my time, as if I was a reader, voraciously reading until the chapter closed with a cliffhanger that only the dawn could resolve.

Now, as I sit within the suffocating confines of my cell, the memory of that encounter coiled around my heart like a thick, black serpent squeezing tight. I know now that I am caught. Caught between a fanged devil and a cliff overlooking a deep blue sea full of great white sharks that make the original movie version look like an anime kitten in a pink scarf.

And I know that with every word I write, there remains a death sentence for those who still dare to dream of dawn.

The pine-needle carpet crunched underfoot, a sound so ordinary yet thunderous in the silence of the Blue Ridge stronghold. A scent like earth's very breath filled my nostrils, the air pregnant with the solemnity of the trees standing sentinel over our clandestine rebellion. They had watched us grow from scattered survivors into a force that dared to challenge the night.

I pressed my back against the rough bark of an ancient oak, the coolness of it seeping through the thin fabric of my jacket. The forest had been our ally, our shroud against the piercing eyes of the empire. But on that day, as the horizon bled crimson, I felt its betrayal. My heart raced — a drumbeat of impending doom — as I scanned the treeline for signs of the enemy we knew was coming.

"Prepare yourselves," I whispered, more to myself than to the shadowy figures around me. Tommy and Danny, my sons, the only family I had left, stood among them, their faces set in grim determination. A foe who knew neither mercy nor fatigue, outnumbered and outflanked us.

Their arrival was a silent tempest, a whirlwind of black cloaks, red robes, and gleaming fangs. Pilatus led them, his presence commanding even amidst the chaos. They descended upon us with the relentlessness and determination of an invading army, their assault a bloody violence that tore through our ranks like death's sharp scythe.

We fought — oh, how we fought — with every ounce of our fading humanity. The clash of steel, the scent of blood, the occasional gunshot, using the last of our ammunition mingled with the cries of the fallen ... on both sides.

Yes, we could kill Them, but not as easily as They could kill us.

That last night for me was a roiling storm of desperation, a battle not just for life, but for the soul of a world teetering on the brink of eternal damnation.

They seized me as the dawn light crept across the battlefield; the ground hallowed by the bodies of those who had stood beside me.

My capture was not simply the ensnaring of one woman: Sage Steel, the progenitor, the one who paved the way for their victory over mankind. Little did they know it was the quelling of "The Wraith". The symbol of hope for all who yearned for freedom from the Crimson Empire's relentless grip.

I remember the weight of their hands on my arms, the cold leer in Pilatus's eyes as he leaned in close, his long, black hair flowing across my shoulder, his fanged mouth expelling a soft breath, a hiss of triumph with just a subtle hint of blood-scent.

"You are mine now, Sage Steel," he murmured, sealing my fate.

And with that simple remark, the rebellion's heart shattered, leaving only whispers of resistance in its wake.

As my mind returned to the present, my fingers hovered over the keys, the dim glow of the laptop screen a lone beacon in the oppressive darkness of my cell. My heart hammered against my ribs, a reminder of the ever-present threat lurking beyond these stone walls. The sharp click of approaching footsteps snapped me back to the present, a jolt of adrenaline coursing through my veins.

Victor.

I typed rapidly, my last message a lifeline cast into the digital abyss.

"They don't know everything." The words flickered on the screen before I slammed the laptop shut, my pulse racing.

The door creaked open, and Victor stepped into the cell, his silhouette a dark smudge against the faint light from the corridor. His face remained unreadable, betraying nothing of his thoughts or intentions.

"Time to rest," he intoned, the words hanging heavy in the air.

"Of course," I replied, my voice steady despite the tremor in my soul.

As he turned to leave, I caught the briefest glint of something unspoken in his gaze — a question, perhaps, or a flicker of doubt. But then it vanished, leaving me isolated once again, enveloped by the silence and the burden of uncertainty.

Outside, the cathedral stood stoic, its spires reaching for a sky shrouded in the malaise of our new reality. Inside, I clung to the fragile thread of hope that my words had found their mark.

Tomorrow, I would write again. Tomorrow, I would fight in the only way left to me.

But now ... now; the shadows held sway, and I could only wait, wondering what the next day would bring me in my personal nightmare of darkness and defiance.

CAPTIVITY:
NIGHTMARE'S BITCH

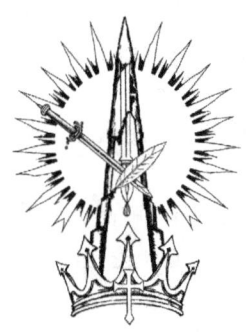

A YELP PIERCES THE silence, and I'm jolted awake. The nightmare clings to me; fangs sinking deep, blood chilling in my veins even as it spills warm over spectral hands. My heart hammers against my ribcage, a frantic drumbeat in the oppressive quiet of the cathedral's underbelly.

The Washington National Cathedral, once a beacon of faith, now looms as a mausoleum of power for those who've claimed the night as their empire. Its grandiose arches are nothing but hollow bones in this new era of darkness. I shiver, not just from the cold that seems to rise from the ancient stone floor, but from the void that has become my world.

I wrap my arms around myself, feeling the press of cold metal against my wrists — shackles that aren't there, save for in memories that flit too close to the surface. The air is damp, heavy with the scent of mildew and the iron tang of fear that never dissipates from this place. Shadows cling to the corners like cobwebs, an extension of the dark that the fangers so adore.

My cell is more tomb than room, a spartan space furnished with only the necessities: a bed that offers no comfort, a small desk, and, surprisingly, a laptop computer, complete with high-speed internet connection — a tool and a tether. The screen casts a pallid glow, a ghost that watches me with an unblinking eye. It's here that I write, weaving words into narratives that twist the truth just enough to satisfy them while leaving breadcrumbs for those who dare to question.

My posting platform is FaceFang, that corruption of what we humans used to chat with Grandma and watch cat videos. They love it just as much as we did. Of course, we have known about Their fascination with social media for a long time now; it was clear since before the attack.

How do I know?

The Wraith, remember?

Besides the small number of troops that fell under my command, I had a whole cadre of hackers at my disposal.

Hacktivists. They were hell against pedophile and rape websites on the darknet back in the day, so you can imagine how they have used the fangers' obsession with our technical toys against them.

My hacktivists have even been able to breach the D.C. closed circuit television cameras several times. Yeah, They catch them eventually and block the feed; but my guys just get right back in.

My hacktivists have never been breached, either. It seems the fangers suck at backhacking; and They have never even caught the monitoring feed on FaceFang. Which is excellent, because my coded messages are right out in the open for everyone to see.

And bonus! They look like they are coming straight from El Supremo Pilatus himself.

Yeah, the fangers, They like the tech, but They are not very good at securing it. At least not yet.

I must admit that Pilatus is not only a devious fuck, but he's also brilliantly smart. He makes the previous human government look like swimmers in the kiddie pool when it comes to using vampire social media for surveillance and the spread of propaganda among his fangers. It's like the treatises and stories that he has me write, all centered on the brave, generous (and in my opinion, vainglorious) Blood Monarch, who, of course, is Pilatus himself.

My fingers dance across the keyboard, the clacking keys a staccato rhythm jiving with the distant murmurs and tapping, marching bootsteps in the stone hall.

Night Sentinels, the fangers call them, but they're elite troops, much like Nazi Sturmtruppen, protecting the emperor and the court, and of course they are my jailers. And worse still, they are enforcers of the silence suffocating us all. Fangers and humans alike. Since my incarceration here, I realize everyone is terrified of them; even the fangers here at court, and they are the privileged few.

Their voices, when they rise and fall through the stone corridors, are reminders that there is a world outside these stone walls — a world I fight to keep alive and free from my place inside.

Each day bleeds into the next, undisturbed save for the artificial twilight that my captors generously bestow. The musty air fills my lungs, and I taste the dust of centuries, of prayers and pleas that people have long since abandoned. I capture every sensation — the chill that seeps into my bones, the rough texture of the stone beneath my fingertips, the faint flicker of desperation that fuels my resolve.

This defiance is my rebellion, my silent war waged in the shadows. With each word I type, each sentence I craft, I hold on to the sliver of self that refuses to be extinguished. They may have ensnared my body in this desolate place, but my spirit, my will, remains untamed.

I am still me.

Still Sage Steel.

Still The Wraith.

I pause, my gaze drifting toward the door that seals me in this stone cage. Beyond it lies uncertainty, a future shrouded in darkness and threaded with peril. And yet, hope flickers — a flame persisting amidst the tempest — fed by sheer willpower alone.

With a sigh that tastes of regret, I turn back to my work, to the stories that are both my weapon and my solace. For now, they are enough. But as the screen's glow fades and I am left once again in the dimness, I know that my fate has a shelf life.

How much longer can I cling to the line between compliance and resistance before it snaps, leaving me to fall into the abyss?

The heavy click of the lock announces his presence before I see him.

The door swings open with a creak that's become all too familiar, and in strides Praetor Pilatus, his cold, piercing gaze locking on mine.

"Miss Steel," he begins, his voice, always so polite, is smooth as the silk lining of his dark, tailored coat. "Your latest piece ... it was quite moving. It received much engagement."

"Thank you, Praetor," I reply, my tone even, betraying none of the turmoil brewing within. His praise is a double-edged sword, and I handle it with care.

He saunters closer, his eyes never leaving my face. There's an elegance to his movements that belies the predator beneath, a grace that's unsettling in its precision.

"However," he continues, leaning against the stone wall with deceptive casualness, "I believe we could further illuminate the nobility of our kind. Perhaps a touch more ... grandeur in your descriptions?"

His suggestion hangs between us, a veiled command wrapped in velvet.

I meet his gaze, my own unflinching.

"Of course," I concede with a careful nod. "The vampires' resilience is indeed a tale worth telling."

Pilatus smiles, but there's no warmth in it. It's the smile of a chess player who believes they've just cornered their opponent's king.

"Indeed," he muses, circling behind my chair as if he were a shark, who, after scenting blood in the water, has taken his position below his prey, readying himself to breach the water with his prey clenched tightly in his jaws. "But let's not forget their sacrifices," he whispers in my ear, and though I fight to hide it, my body stiffens, paralyzed in fear. "Their eternal struggle against misunderstanding and prejudice. You do understand, don't you?" His whisper continues, and I feel the coolness of his lips lightly brush the lobe of my ear.

"Perfectly," I assure him, my stomach flipping in disgust, though at the same time my mind races, searching for the line between appeasement and truth. To write their fictionalized history as they demand is to deny the blood spilled, the freedoms crushed underfoot.

Yet to challenge them openly is to invite destruction.

"Good." His approval feels like a coffin shroud settling over me. "I look forward to your next submission."

"May I ask," I venture cautiously, seizing the moment to glean some shred of insight, "about your past, Praetor? For authenticity's sake, you see. All fiction writers research historic events, even if they don't use the event in their writing. It helps to give them an understanding of the experience, and it lends depth to the narrative. You could be my search engine into vampire history, instead of me just making it up out of sackcloth and ashes."

He moves to the side, and I turn my head just enough to meet his icy blue eyes. It's like looking into the eyes of a reptile, cold, unfeeling, and deadly.

Pilatus pauses, his eyes narrowing subtly.

"My past?" He echoes, a flicker of something — amusement or suspicion — crossing his cold features. "A curious request. But why not? Knowledge, after all, is power. But an investment in knowledge pays the best interest."

"Exactly," I breathe, relieved yet wary.

This is a dance on a knife's edge, and one misstep could prove fatal.

"Very well," he agrees, straightening to his full, imposing height. "Next time, Miss Steel. We shall delve into my history together."

"Next time," I echo as he turns on his heel and strides out, the heavy door closing with a definitive thud behind him.

Alone once more, I'm left to ponder the enigma that is Pilatus, each visit peeling back another layer of the intricate tapestry of lies and truths. What secrets lie in the shadows of his past? And what price will I pay to uncover them?

I shiver, not from the chill of the cell, but from the realization that my defiance, as much as my writing, has drawn the attention of the monster at the heart of this dark empire. With every word I write, I weave my destiny tighter around me — a garment of resistance that may yet be my undoing.

As the silence of the cell presses in around me, I can't shake the feeling that something pivotal looms on the horizon, something that could shatter my fragile balance between capitulation and rebellion. With a sense of foreboding, I stare at the door, wondering what darkness the next visit will bring.

And as the Cathedral's shadows lengthen, I am left with the echoing click of the lock to my jail cell and the haunting question:

How much longer until the darkness claims me completely?

As Pilatus's silhouette recedes into the gloom, his departure as silent and unnerving as a ghost vanishing at daybreak. The echo of his soft footsteps fade, replaced by the heavy clank of another set of boots.

His heavy boots always alert me to his approach, as if sounding a warning and giving me time to collect myself.

Deliberate action might merit gratitude, though I suspect simple dullness is the cause.

Victor enters, his presence an unspoken reminder of the vampires' omnipotence within these hallowed walls.

He surveys me with those inscrutable eyes, a statue carved from the same cold stone that encases my world. I am not sure what he is looking for and I can't decipher his thoughts; no flicker of emotion betrays whether he's friend or foe, mere jailer or silent ally. For a heartbeat, we share this cryptic communion before he too departs, the reverberating slam of the door sealing my solitude.

I sink onto the sparse bed, the mattress hardly yielding beneath my weight. The chill from the stone floor seeps through my thin-soled shoes, wrapping around my bones like the fingers of a long-forgotten lover — intimate, but unwelcome. A shudder courses through me, not only from Pilatus's thinly veiled threats, but from the burgeoning realization of how precariously I teeter on the knife-edge of survival.

I would never have volunteered for such a post; but even I had to admit that my capture was beneficial to the resistance in many ways.

Pilatus wanted me because he had used my writing as a false reality in his worldwide conquest. He didn't even realize the amount of damage that he had done to the U. S. resistance and he probably wouldn't care if he knew.

He never saw us as much of a threat to begin with.

He just wanted the writer that had been his inspiration for the recorder of their history.

He was at heart, a fan.

A fucking terrifying, ultra dangerous, psychotic fan; but a fan, nonetheless.

The question was, what could I do to use that to help the humans beyond what I had been able to feed them?

I stood and paced my sparse cell, rubbing my face in thought.

In the oppressive silence that followed, my mind raced.

Each word I craft in my forced labor is a word of deceit, yet it's also a strand in my web of resistance. I have been able to send information to the resistance about the resources here and what I overhear about issues in other parts of the empire.

Can I continue to toe this perilous line?

To paint their world in strokes of truth laced with defiance?

I look through the barred portal of my cell door.

A bitter taste coats my tongue — a taste I am too familiar with — the tang of iron and fear. My own pulse throbs in my ears, a harsh rhythm that sounds too much like a countdown.

Every second in this cathedral-turned-prison, every breath drawn in the shadow of the Night Sentinels, brings me closer to the cliff's edge from which, one day, I may topple.

The dim light in the stone hall casts monstrous shadows across the walls, devilish figures that dance in a ghoulish display.

They're omens, perhaps, or simply the product of a mind fraying at the edges.

My fingers curl into fists, nails biting into palms — a futile attempt to anchor myself with pain to the reality of my cell, rather than the terrors that lurk in my imagination.

"Will I become one of your tragic heroes, Pilatus?" I whisper into the void, my voice a hollow sound amidst the cathedral's vastness.

"Or am I destined to be a footnote in your grand narrative of revisionist history?"

No answer comes, only the faintest drip of water somewhere in the distance — a metronome marking the passage of time in a place where dawn never breaks. I pace the confines of my cage once more, each step a silent rebellion against the inertia that threatens to consume me.

I stop once more at the windowless aperture of the door that serves as my only visual portal to the world beyond. Here, I press my forehead against the icy stone of the wall in which the door is set. I close my eyes against the darkness that seeks to engulf me. The question of my resistance hangs suspended in the air, as tangible as the bars that cage me.

In the stillness, a resolve solidifies within my chest, hard and unyielding. I will write their stories, yes, but in my own words, with my own truths woven between the lines.

Someday, if fortune truly favors the bold, my tales will be the undoing of their empire — the same words that once carved its bloody foundation.

And with that thought, I moved away from the barred opening, retreating into the shadows of my cell, knowing that my existence teeters on the brink of revelation or ruin.

For now, I still know who I am.

I am Sage Steel, author, rebel leader, and captive, standing alone against the Emperor of Nightmares.

But tomorrow? And the tomorrow after that?

Even a wretch like me knows that as long as my heart beats, the future will always remain unwritten.

WORDS ETCHED IN BLOOD

SAGE'S FINGERS DANCED OVER the keys, the only sound in her cramped cell save for the low hum of machinery buried within the cathedral's walls. Her laptop cast a harsh blue light across her features, etching deep shadows that flickered and swayed with each new line of text. Above, in the cathedral proper, the vaulted ceilings stretched into darkness, a silent witness to her rebellion.

"Remember the Alamo, Sam Houston said, fully embracing his vampire nature," she typed, embedding instructions for an assault on a vampire supply depot outside of Houston, Texas, within the historical account.

The words felt like a prayer, each keystroke a plea for freedom, a thread weaving together the tattered remnants of human resistance.

Outside, the night blanketed Washington D.C., muffling the sounds of the undead patrols that roamed the streets. Sage's heart raced as she imagined Tommy and Danny huddled around their own screen miles away, deciphering her veiled guidance.

In the Blue Ridge Mountains, a soft ping echoed through the hidden control room of the resistance base camp, as Tommy's computer received the incoming decoded message from the hacktivists that were so loyal to his mother. He exchanged a glance with Danny, a shared spark of anticipation in their eyes before they buried themselves in the task of translation.

Fans whirred, circulating the air in the command bunker. Maps cluttered the tabletops, radios crackled, and screens flickered with surveillance footage — a testament to the hope still flickering amidst the human's despair.

"Look here," Tommy whispered, pointing to a phrase nestled innocuously between lines about historical battle strategy. "The 'unexpected snow in April' — it's a weak spot in the northern sector."

Danny leaned closer, the scent of pine and damp earth from his worn jacket mingling with the musty air of the command center. His fingers traced routes on a map, plotting a course based on their mother's insights. They both knew the gravity of the information, the lives that hung in the balance.

"Mom's risking everything," Danny murmured, his youthful voice barely audible above the soft whir of machines. His admiration for her was palpable, a beacon of hope in what seemed the endless night of their struggle. "And as much as I appreciate that, we got to find out where they have her. We have to get her the hell out of there before they figure out who she really is and start torturing her for information. Once that starts, we are all fucked! No one person knows more about operations in the resistance than she does."

"She'd die before she spilled." Tommy, always the older brother, his voice a deep river, steady and sure, coursing through the landscape of the command center like a beacon of hope amidst the chaos. It was the voice of a warrior, unshaken by fear, and filled with the resolute determination to save their mother and their cause.

"Nobody can withstand torture, Tommy." Danny mumbled.

"Danny, if she spilled, she'd be signing our death warrants. She'd die before she'd do that." Tommy gave him a harsh glance. "Besides, if she wanted us to risk it, she'd have let us know where she was. Even the hackers are having a problem tracking down her location beyond D.C. They think that is intentional; on her part." He looked once more at the map. "Eventually they will pinpoint her location and we will go in and get her. But not because we are scared that she will spill — because we need her. We need The Wraith."

Their connection to Sage was more than filial; it was the lifeline of the entire rebellion. And so, with hushed voices, they pulled up the satellite surveillance maps of the Houston area. They planned their next move, guided by the silent words of their mother, echoing through the digital void.

Pilatus, draped in a black and crimson robe that swallowed the light around him, stopped pacing. The grand chamber, with its ornate tapestries and ancient stone, resonated with the hum of tension. His eyes flowed over the typewritten words of a report and his lips thinned in irritation. He extended a pale hand, the veins like dark rivers beneath alabaster skin, and beckoned to the underling who had brought him the report — a vampire whose eyes flickered under the weight of his master's gaze.

"Keep her under watch," Pilatus commanded, his voice cutting through the silence with the precision of a blade. "I want everything recorded. Every word, every sigh — nothing escapes us. She is up to something; and I will know what it is." His icy blue eyes returned to the printout before him, searching for what lay hidden between the lines of Sage's careful prose.

The underling bowed low, his nose well below his knees, his servility betraying his fear, then scurried away like a rat to dispatch additional surveillance to the cell where Sage wove her dangerous tales.

Sage's heart pounded as she jolted awake from her nightmare, the taste of terror still bitter on her tongue. Sage sat up in bed, gasping for air as the nightmare faded away. Her vision blurred with tears and sweat dripped from her forehead, stinging her eyes. Her heart raced wildly against her ribcage and her chest heaved with shallow breaths as she struggled to catch her bearings once more. She was alone in her small, dimly lit cell; but the memory of the vampire fangs still lingered in every pore of her being. It felt as though they were sunk deep into her flesh, a mouth working against her flesh to suck out every last drop of her blood as she writhed helplessly under their assault.

She could still feel the icy touch of their hands against her neck, the strength of their long, wet tongue tracing the line of her collarbones as they supped upon her life force. The memory of the smell of fresh blood filled the surrounding air, making it difficult to breathe; even the lingering scent of lavender on her pillowcase couldn't mask the coppery tang that hung thick like a fog in her mind.

Like an unwelcome visitor, the nightmare haunted, leaving behind images of terror and desperation.

She remembered running through endless corridors covered in shadows, trying to escape their grasp; feeling their icy hands brush past her skin as she dodged around corners and through doors. The sound of their footsteps echoed off the walls with each step they took towards her, growing louder with every passing second.

Their voices whispered promises of doom and death in lost languages, but understandable all too well by Sage's tormented subconsciousness.

She swore she could still hear them laughing dementedly behind her, snarling at every missed turn or hesitation on her part as they hunted her.

Her heart continued to pound in her ears even after she realized she was safe — it took several long moments before its frantic rhythm finally slowed back down to something resembling a normal pace.

Sweat chilled on her skin when it met the cool air of the cell, sending shivers down her spine that nothing could seem to quell.

Every movement seemed sluggish now; moving felt like wading through the mud of a swamp as adrenaline gradually drained away like sand from an hourglass emptying its grains one by one.

Tears streamed down Sage's cheeks unchecked as she curled into a ball on top of crumpled sheets dampened by more than just perspiration alone — fear mingled with despair, painting a grim picture in her mind.

"It wasn't real," she whispered hoarsely to herself between shuddering breaths; words more prayer than reassurance.

But deep down inside, she knew better: this wasn't some random nightmare spawned from late-night horror films or even an overwrought imagination; it held too much personal meaning for that comforting excuse.

No ... this was something else — something more horrific.

As if Pilatus himself had entered her mind to cause havoc.

In the throne room, amidst vampires who watched her like hungry hawks circling their prey, Sage tried to project an image of humble servitude while her mind raced with subterfuge.

"Come, sit at my feet. You may ask your questions, and we ... will talk about the past." Pilatus ordered, his voice resonating through the cavernous space, as he motioned to a spot directly in front of his throne.

She hesitated, her plea about aching knees escaping her lips with a whisper, when a guard loomed over her, his grip tightening on her shoulder like a vise.

But before she could be forced down, Pilatus was upon the guard, a blur of motion too swift for human eyes.

A sickening, fleshy rip echoed, and blood splattered across the floor, across Sage.

The guard's scream died in his throat as he collapsed to his knees, clutching the stump of his shoulder, attempting to stem the spurts of black blood from his body; as he stared at the arm in Pilatus's grasp.

His arm torn from his body by his own lord's fury.

The guard's eyes swiftly looked at the bloody floor as Pilatus glared down at him before tossing the guard's own arm back to him.

As Pilatus looked at her, Sage's breath froze in her chest.

"Let this be a lesson," Pilatus declared loudly to the court, his eyes never leaving Sage's shocked face. "No one touches what is mine." The Vampire Emperor stepped close to murmur, "You may return to your cell to wash, Miss Steel."

He motioned to Victor, who stepped forward to escort her away.

Sage's hands trembled as she hurried back to her dim cell, her heart pounding in her chest. Her footsteps echoed against the cold stone floor, and every shadow in the corridor seemed to loom larger than life. Behind her, Victor, ever silent, followed, his presence a constant reminder of the tense confrontation they'd just endured. Though he kept his distance, the air between them was thick with unspoken words and a shared unease, the gravity of their recent encounter with Pilatus pressing down upon them like a lead cloak.

The new camera's red light blinked ominously from the ceiling corner of her cell, reminding her that her every move was now shadowed by the threat of discovery. The keyboard clacked under her fingers as she composed her next message, fraught with peril yet indispensable to the rebellion.

"Safe for now," she typed, the words a lifeline in the darkness. Her thoughts spun with strategy and fear, her resolve hardening against the dread of what she had seen. Each letter on the screen was a waltz with danger, each sentence a step and swing of her hips closer to salvation — or doom.

Tommy, Danny, the names talismans in her mind against the encroaching despair. *I'll keep you safe, no matter the cost.*

The door creaked open with sudden abruptness, and Victor's tall figure loomed in the doorway, his presence casting a long shadow across the stark cell. Sage's heart raced as she automatically minimized the messaging application on the darknet, her fingers trembling but her face a mask of composure.

"Working late, Miss Steel?" Victor's voice was cool, detached, yet there was an edge to it that suggested a predator circling its prey.

"Just some additional notes on the cathedral's history," Sage replied evenly, pushing back her fear and surprise at the smooth voice of the normally silent praetorian guard. She gestured towards the screen, which now displayed a benign document filled with historical dates and architectural terms.

Victor took a step closer, his eyes narrowing as he peered at the laptop's display. "Pilatus grows weary of secrets," he said after a moment, his tone carrying a veiled threat. "I urge you to remember your place here."

"Of course," she responded, her throat dry. "I have no interest in secrets, only in my work."

Victor held her gaze for a beat longer, searching for any hint of deception.

Finally, with a curt nod, he turned on his heel and exited the cell. His parting words hung heavy in the air. "Be careful, Miss Steel. The walls have eyes, and the shadows talk."

The harsh, metallic sound of the cell door slamming shut reverberated through the chilly air, a grim reminder of my captivity.

I let out a breath I hadn't noticed I'd been holding in, my heart pounding like a war drum in my chest. Every tick of the clock was a countdown to potential discovery and disaster.

The soft chime from my computer sliced through the silence like a knife.

A new message had arrived.

As I decoded the cryptic lines from Tommy and Danny via my hacktivist network, an icy dread seeped into my veins, coating my soul with frost.

There is a traitor among us? The very thought sent tremors of panic coursing through me, threatening to shatter the human's fragile resistance from within.

Humans who betrayed other humans to the vampires were the worst of the worst; caring for nothing beyond themselves. Filthy cowards who were self-loathing, race-traitors, who cared nothing for the future of the world or their own species, or anything beyond their own life span.

The Resistance hated these race-traitors even more than the fangers, their vampire overlords.

At least the fangers had a purpose amongst themselves. At least those bloodsuckers were driven by a primal instinct. Of course, their purpose was to feed off humans like humans fed on cattle.

It was a twisted, fucked-up purpose, but it still revolved around their survival.

But race-traitors?

Race-traitors would sell out their own mother to secure an easier life for themselves; or the hope they would be the last 'moo-er' in the chute.

"Who can you trust?" My fingers danced across the keyboard with frantic urgency, each press of the keys echoing my rising fear.

"Be alert. We trust no one. We will find the traitor," came the stark reply minutes later.

My pulse thundered in my ears as I navigated this treacherous landscape of suspicion and deceit with each coded message sent out into the ether.

If Pilatus discovered what I was doing, it wouldn't just be me he'd come after — Tommy and Danny were just as much in his crosshairs. With each keystroke, I wove a perilous path through a minefield of suspicion and betrayal.

The blinking red light of the ever-watchful camera in the corner served as a chilling reminder that peril lurked around every corner, the dead gaze of its lens boring into me like a frozen blade, always there and always ready to cut down anything in its path.

At an unexpected sound outside my cell door, adrenaline surged through me and I slammed the computer shut, extinguishing its dim light and my connection to my children.

Submerged in darkness once again, anxiety twisted knots in my stomach while determination steeled my resolve.

Stay strong echoed in my mind as the oppressive silence of my prison cell enveloped me, the weight of the unseen future crushing down upon my chest, like I was being tortured with the *peine forte et dure*, one stone after another placed upon my chest until I entered a plea or died.

Each passing moment added another stone to the pile.

Stay strong — for them.

THE TERRIFYING UNVEILING OF THE BLOOD MONARCH

THE HEAVY OAK DOOR groaned on its ancient hinges as I stepped into the grand chamber, the scent of beeswax and time-worn stone permeating the air. Shadows danced along the walls, thrown by the flickering candles that held back the darkness with their feeble light. Pilatus lounged upon his throne, a silhouette carved from night itself, eyes gleaming like twin shards of blue ice. Their piercing gaze tracked my cautious approach, dissecting my every move.

"Ah, Sage," he purred, the sound echoing off the high vaulted ceiling. "You've arrived."

I swallowed hard, the weight of uncertainty pressing down on me like the stones above. At the sounds of the double doors to the throne room closing behind me, I turned around to see that Victor was gone, and even more unusual, the entire chamber was empty except for the two of us.

I guess he had dispensed with the formalities in our privacy.

Fine. Sage, it would be. But perhaps he will get more than he bargained for.

Perhaps he will get The Wraith.

The chill in the room wasn't just from the draft; it crept into my bones, a harbinger of something bloody and dangerous that awaited.

"I take it you do not fear that I will try to end your existence." It was a statement, not a question. I walked to the front of the dais to look up at the monster before me.

If the moment to die had arrived, I would confront it with courage.

His eyes flashed red before he smirked and shook his head slowly. Then he rose from the throne and walked down the dais to stand before me; to tower over me.

I knew he was ancient. Reputed to be the first of his kind. He was the strongest to declare himself emperor over the entire world.

Still, if he had ever been human, he must have been a giant amongst his people.

Hell, he was still a giant amongst modern man.

"Your majesty required an audience?" It was a snarky question, bold in its asking, though my voice betrayed me, quivering slightly as I looked up into his cold, cold eyes.

"Indeed," he replied, steepling his fingers with calculated grace. His lips curled into a smile that never reached those glacial eyes. "It's time you heard the tale of our beginning—the true ... genesis ... of our empire."

The candles sputtered as if protesting the story they were about to illuminate. I felt an icy knot tightening in my stomach, the cold spreading throughout my entrails as I sensed the gravity of what was to come.

"Walk with me, Sage." He said and motioned with his hand toward the back of the throne room.

The change in his address put me on my guard. And though I was tempted, I would be a fool to challenge him over it. He was incredibly lethal and volatile; the most dangerous Fanger I had ever come across.

"So, I am glad to see that the floor in front of your throne suffered so little from the excess of blood when you ripped off the guard's arm the other day." I remarked coolly.

God, what was I thinking?

The realization hit me like lightning, frying my already frayed nerves, sending them into a spiral of disorientation. My mind, worn down by the endless days and nights of captivity, was losing its grasp on reality, allowing me to say things that could only be certifiable. But in this twisted court, where a monster sat on a throne and a human was reduced to a pet, it seemed almost natural to tease the dangerous being before me.

As his cold eyes bore into mine, I couldn't help but wonder if I had finally lost my mind.

"Are you still upset about that, Sage?" The psychopath replied. "Don't worry, you tender-hearted creature ... it will grow back," he reassured me, his voice gentle and soothing. He gripped my hand suddenly, his fingers tight around mine, his touch surprisingly warm. It was as if I was a lost child in need of guidance, his grip leading me through uncertain territory. "This way, Sage."

I must admit, this familiarity from this monster fucking pissed me off.

I am far from stupid; but sometimes, I do stupid things.

But not right now. I clenched my jaw, the sharp taste of blood mingling with the metallic tang in my mouth as I pressed my teeth into the soft flesh of my cheek, desperate to silence the stream of foolish words that threatened to escape.

I followed him into an antechamber and then through double doors that led into what was obviously his personal rooms. He motioned to a table laden with meats and fruits.

I shook my head.

He released me and walked over to the table and picked up a copper pitcher.

"Wine?" He asked.

"I am not thirsty." I answered quietly.

It was a lie. I was parched. But I would desiccate and blow away before I would drink with this monster.

"I see." He stated quietly. "Victor tells me you have stopped eating or drinking." He poured himself a goblet of what looked to be wine. "Are you trying to harm yourself, Sage? You know I will not allow that to happen."

"I will eat when I am hungry, and drink when I thirst." I told him coldly.

His eyes narrowed at me in irritation. "Fine. Then you can watch me while I eat." He motioned to an oversized sofa. "Sit."

Does he think I'm a dog? I threw him a glare before gently lowering myself into a sitting position.

Oh, it was heaven. It had been so long since I had sat on something remotely comfortable.

I began to sigh in pleasure and then realized that he was watching me intently. I glared at him and he gave me an evil grin, as if he knew exactly what I was feeling.

He picked up a piece of white meat from a bronze platter with his fingers and hungrily bit into it.

I was clueless about what it was. It could have been turkey or goose.

I just hoped it wasn't long pork.

I swallowed, and then said, "I am surprised that you eat anything at all."

"Living beings must consume to survive. It is a fallacy for you to think that we are dead, Sage." He told me before slowly licking grease from his fingers.

"You're not?" I quipped.

"Well, you've killed us. For something to be killed, I declare it must first be alive." Ice dripped from his words as he remembered my crimes.

I stayed quiet. This monster was too crafty by half.

"What is it you wanted to tell me, Pilatus?" I finally asked.

He motioned with his hand, and a servant that I had not noticed stepped from the shadows of the room, startling me.

I watched him as he walked out the double doors, closing them behind; shutting me in with this monster ... alone.

"I would begin with telling you my birth name." He said, and I looked at him in surprise. "My birth name is Pontius Pilate."

My mouth dropped open and I couldn't stop myself from bursting out, "You lie! I remember my catechism. Pontius Pilate committed suicide after the crucifixion of Christ."

"Such propaganda. Such truths and lies you humans have." He said with a twist of his firm lips. "You see me before you. I am very much alive. And I am Pontius Pilate."

He came and sat in a chair across from the sofa as I continued to stare at him in disbelief.

"Long before the world knew of our kind," Pilatus began, his voice smooth as silk and just as dangerous, "there were three of us — Ananos, a Jewish High Priest, Herod Antipas, you may remember him as the beheader of John the Baptist, and of course, myself. We were all powerful mortals, but we were hungry for power beyond the grasp of death. We sought magic and supernatural power, and in our quest, we found the opportunity in a man who was performing the most wondrous miracles throughout our land. The people called this man Jesus Christ."

A shiver ran through me, an instinctual repulsion at the blasphemy his words suggested. The shadows seemed to lean in closer, eager to hear the confession of their master.

"We three plotted and strategized, stirring up the community against this upstart Christ who claimed to be the messiah. He made it easy, actually. Christ was too tolerant, dining with sinners, whores, and tax collectors. He broke the Jewish Sabbath and referred to their God as 'Father', claiming to be his son." His tone was mocking, as if even now, after over two millennia, he couldn't believe Christ's stupidity in such overt claims.

"His crucifixion," Pilatus continued, each word wrapped in dark amusement, "was not merely the ending of a prophet it was an act of ambition, but not sin. You see, we tortured him to find out his source of magic because we wanted it for ourselves. He never told us the source, and so we put him to death; exacting revenge for his silence and pleasing the populace. But, little did we know, that his crucifixion would be the birth of gods among men."

I struggled to breathe, the air thickening with each horrific truth unveiled.

"You look pale, my dear. Are you sure you aren't thirsty?" He asked solicitously, offering me his own goblet.

Smelling the wine and blood mixture, I swallowed hard, keeping bile from exploding from my mouth, and shook my head, leaning away from the outstretched goblet.

"So, for your part in the crucifixion, God cursed you?" I managed to ask without puking all over the floor.

A harsh, blood-scented laugh crashed from his mouth. "Cursed? Heavens no, my Sage! Do I look cursed? I am the emperor of the world! I am the Blood Monarch." His laughter died down gradually as I cringed away from his madness. "This," he motioned from his head to his feet, "was an intentional act."

I looked at him in confusion.

"You say you remember your catechism. Do you remember the centurion who pierced Christ's side with a spear? Do you know why he did it?" He asked.

I remembered about the spear in Jesus's side, but I couldn't find my voice while looking into his wide icy eyes as he stared evilly at me, so I shook my head silently; unable to pull my eyes from his.

"People in that time practiced crurifragium, or the breaking of one's legs below the knee, was done to speed up the process of death during crucifixion. But when the centurions approached Christ on the cross, they found he was already dead. But, to make sure that he was truly dead, a centurion named Longinus pierced his side and was bathed in a shower of his entrails and blood." He looked at my horrified expression with a cool glance of his own before continuing.

"Longinus suffered from a diseased eye that, after being touched by the blood of Christ, was cured. You can imagine our excitement when he presented himself that night and told us of this miraculous happening. We had Christ's body exhumed from his cave-like tomb under the cover of night. We did not roll his tomb's stone back into place, but left Longinus to 'guard' the opened tomb. In reality, he was tasked with spying on other radicals who might visit the tomb of their messiah."

Pilatus stood and rounded the couch, pulling me against the back of the sofa, and I froze in fear as he leaned down to whisper roughly in my ear, "We brought Christ back to my palace, cut his body into pieces, ate his flesh and drank his blood. And became what you see now."

My lungs failed to function, and my breathing stopped as I tried to absorb his words.

The foundation of this empire, this ageless monstrosity, rested upon betrayal so profound and actions so horrific that they threatened to shatter my understanding of all I thought immutable.

"It's a lie." I whispered. "He rose from the dead and lived amongst his followers for 40 days, teaching and ministering to his disciples. And then God called him home, he ascended to heaven."

"Yes, yes, propaganda was alive and well in that time, too. Much of it fostered by us, you should know. It is true, Jesus' followers did mourn him as a martyr. And created many stories about him. After all, man has known well before Machiavelli existed that anything, be it immoral or unethical, such as lies, violence, or even murder, can be justified if the goal is important enough." Pilatus said, a hint of mockery lacing his tone.

"To them, the end justified the lies. But we ... Ananos, Herod, and myself ... the three of us ... we celebrated Christ truthfully, though only to a very few, as the key to our ascension." He whispered against my skin.

I stiffened once more as I felt him sniff my neck like a bloodhound takes to a tracking scent.

"Still don't believe me, my Sage? Where do you think your act of communion comes from? *Whoever eats my flesh and drinks my blood remains in me and I in him,* John 6:56. Our mortal and corruptible natures are transformed by being joined to the source of life through the eating of the body and drinking the blood of Christ."

The horrors of history, twisted into a perverse origin story, clawed bloody grooves into my mind, and I struggled to find purchase against the revulsion that fought back.

This was the legacy of the vampire empire — a sacrilege so deep it tainted every shadow in the room.

"Is this supposed to impress me?" I choked out, my horror morphing into a cold blaze of anger. "Your vile actions, justified as ambition?"

"Understanding is not a requirement," he retorted, his relaxed demeanor unshaken by my disgust. "Acceptance, however, is inevitable."

Her hands balled into tight fists, the ominous ambiance enveloping her like a shroud. Her nails dug into her palms as she attempted, in vain, to distance herself from the beast that lurked behind her.

"Speak, Pilatus," Sage urged, her voice quivering with a potent blend of shock and rage. "Where does virtue live in such a monstrous act? How do you rationalize devouring the holy?"

Pilatus's answer was not immediate. He let her go and returned to his regal seat. The wavering candlelight throughout the room cast ominous shadows across his countenance as he sat with the fluidity of a predator.

"Survival," Pilatus murmured, the word rolling off his tongue like a lover's sigh — reverent, but laced with something darker. His eyes, cold as the void between stars, settled on her with a predator's detachment. "For power. For dominion. For eternity — we embraced what had to be done. Brutality was not a choice or sin. It was evolution! It was sacrament!" His lips curled into a knowing smile, as if savoring a memory that spanned centuries.

"You call us monsters," he continued, voice low and measured, each word a blade slicing through the air. "But what are monsters if not the victors of an ancient war? We didn't ask for permission. We didn't beg the gods for favor. We tore destiny and power from their cold, dead body. And what of your humans?" His gaze darkened, contempt seeping into his tone. "When confront with a conquering force, they abandoned the will to survive. They traded blood and fire for chains and prayers. They don't fight anymore. They wait. They hope that mercy will come — as if mercy was ever anything but weakness. Predators don't mourn the prey."

Pilatus stood and paced slowly, his footsteps echoing through the cavernous space, each step a reminder of the weight of millennia. "We claimed eternity not with words ... but with teeth and iron. We didn't hesitate when the world trembled before us. We didn't weep for the lives we consumed. We feasted on eternity while your ancestors cowered in the shadows, praying to gods who had long since been eaten."

He turned, his smile now a cruel echo of triumph. "Supremacy is not inherited. It is seized. We ate the shepherd who would lead the weak, and in his place, we became the wolves who feast upon the flock. We rewrote existence, carved it into flesh and stone, while humans—" His sneer deepened, eyes narrowing to slits. "—grew fat on complacency, too fearful to defend themselves. We carved our empire in blood while your kind forgot how to sharpen a blade."

His voice dropped to a chilling whisper, yet it filled the space as if spoken by a thousand tongues. "And now, your humans dare to dream of rebellion? You speak of freedom while kneeling before the gallows? We built this empire with blood and terror, Sage. Your words may echo through the darkness, but they cannot unmake what was born in sacrifice and sealed with eternity."

A moment of silence hung in the air, thick with the weight of his words. His expression softened — a mask of amusement laced with warning as he sat once more. "The strong do not fear the whispers of the weak. And we ... are destiny."

The tension between them was like two trucks speeding toward each other, a collision between his brutal pragmatism and the moral storm raging within her.

She stood, her 5'9" frame, tall and straight; her backbone like the steel of her family name. The ancient stone beneath her feet seemed to absorb the heat of their conflict, while the air thickened and chilled, extinguishing any residual warmth within the sacred walls.

"Destiny?" Sage's voice was steady, but her eyes burned with defiant rage, meeting his gaze without flinching. A slow, almost mocking smile curved her lips — a dangerous glint of titanium behind her emerald irises. "Is that what you tell yourself when the silence grows too loud? When the echoes of the lives you've stolen scream louder than the prayers of those who fear you?"

She took a deliberate step closer, the distance between them closing like the tightening of a noose. "You speak of eternity, Pilatus," she said softly, her voice laced with venomous certainty. "But eternity is not unchanging. It's a cage. A hollow echo where the screams of the damned never fade."

Her expression hardened, her words now a blade aimed straight at the core of his arrogance. "You call it destiny ... but I see damnation. Not just for you." Her eyes narrowed, the fire in her tone rising. "For every soul you've bound to your empire. Your children. Your followers. They will burn with you."

Her lips curled, voice dropping to a whisper, but the promise in her words was louder than thunder. "You may have rewritten history with blood and lies ... but I will write the end. And when that final chapter is read, your name will not be carved in glory — it will be etched in ash. History won't remember you as anything more than another brutal, bloody, tyrant Pilatus. But it will remember who brought you to your knees."

Pilatus flashed a smile at her defiance - an amusement that reminded her of a predator playing with its prey. For an instant, it shined through the predatory essence of his being — a chilling testament to the darkness, more evil now that she understood it was a corrupted light, sitting before her.

"Those are human worries, Sage," he dismissed with a casual flick of his hand. "Mortal worries. We surpassed such petty concerns long ago. We are immortal."

"But not eternal!" She snapped.

He shrugged as if he didn't care. Her opinion didn't matter.

Her heart hammered in her chest; each throb mirrored the weightiness of this revelation and underscored the philosophical divide that stretched vast between them.

Sage found herself breathless, but choked out another question. "And what price did you pay for this transcendence?"

This time Pilatus's grin faltered ever so slightly, a crack in his otherwise impenetrable façade — before he replied coolly, "A price mere humans could never comprehend. But the treasure was worth any price. The treasure of immortality; an undying existence. To be that of an earthbound God!"

This was the true visage of the vampire empire: ambition unrestrained by morality and survival at the expense of the soul.

"I don't believe you! I don't! You vampires are known for your lies! Look how you used my fiction to get here!" Sage told him in a breathless whisper, denying his words. "Besides, God wouldn't let the flesh of his son sow such corruption. And you would lie just to shock and hurt! You and your kind are a blight on the world!"

"A blight on the world? Consider the chaos of your human world before we took control," Pilatus began again, his voice a lullaby of twisted logic. "The wars, the suffering, your species' continuous need to pollute the planet in the name of progress. Your endless cycle of death and rebirth. We bring order to that chaos. A new age governed by beings of superior strength, wisdom, and longevity."

Sage's fists clenched at her sides, her nails digging bloody crescents into her palms. She could feel the weight of centuries in his words, the heavy drapery of justification cloaking his monstrous deeds.

"Superior?" She questioned, her voice suppressing the storm brewing within her. "Or just more adept at hiding your savagery behind a veneer of civility as long as you are in control?"

"Isn't that what all rulers do, Sage?" Pilatus leaned back, an ancient regality about him as the candlelight danced across the contours of his face. "Dress their intentions in finery so the masses will kneel?"

She wanted to scream, to unleash the horror and revulsion churning inside her, but she knew it would be as effective as hurling pebbles against a fortress.

"According to you, *YOU* have built your monstrous empire on a foundation of betrayal, murder, cannibalism, and blood," Sage said with cold clarity. "You see it as necessary; I see it as tyranny and madness."

"Perspective," he whispered, almost fondly, "is the privilege of gods and monsters."

The atmosphere in the room tightened, constricting around Sage like a noose. The air itself seemed to thicken, heavy with the musty scent of old stone and the iron tang of blood long since spilled.

Then Pilatus leaned forward; the shadows clinging to him as if they were loath to part from his presence. His voice, once commanding, now took on a conspiratorial tone.

"Ah, but we've only scraped the surface of secrets, my dear," he said, his eyes gleaming with the promise of untold depths of knowledge. "There are truths within truths, and lies within lies, layers that would shake the very pillars of heaven and earth if known."

Sage's breath hitched, her mind racing to fathom what darker revelations could lie beneath the already gruesome history of these creatures.

"More?" she echoed, her voice a thin veil over the tremor of fear.

"Much more," Pilatus assured, his whisper like the brush of a tomb's chill. "And in time, you shall know them all."

With that final cryptic promise, the candles snuffed out as if devoured by the darkness itself, plunging the grand chamber — and Sage's heart — into an abyss that threatened to swallow her whole. The silence that followed was pregnant with the unsaid, with the terror of knowledge yet to come.

As the last glimmer of light died away from her sight, Sage stood frozen with the echo of Pilatus's words still floating around the room, feeling the stiff fingers of dread creep up her spine.

The dance of truth and power was far from over.

What more could there be?

What deeper horror could possibly lay buried than that which was already revealed?

THIRTY PIECES OF BLOOD

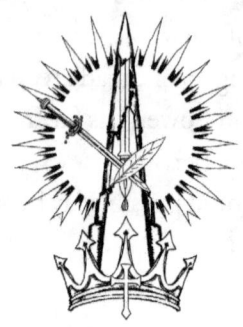

TOMMY STEEL'S FIST CAME down hard on the rickety table, the sharp crack echoing like a gunshot through the bunker's hollow confines. The maps and papers scattered like dead leaves, fluttering to the cold, dirt-packed floor.

"Keep your damn voices down," he hissed, his green eyes — so much like his mother's — sweeping across the grim faces of his fellow rebel leaders. Shadows swallowed the edges of the room, clinging to the stone walls like hungry phantoms. The faint clink of weapons being cleaned echoed like the toll of funeral bells in the oppressive quiet.

They were buried deep in the guts of the Blue Ridge Mountains, where the scent of damp earth mixed with sweat and desperation. But despite the illusion of safety carved into the mountain's flesh, everyone in the room could feel the noose tightening — an invisible grip closing around their throats.

A stone tomb masquerading as a refuge.

Danny stood beside his brother, his jaw clenched so tight it could've cracked bone. His sharp blue eyes scanned the group, watching, weighing. The tension in the room was a living thing, thick and suffocating, seeping into their lungs with each shallow breath.

Fear wasn't just a feeling here — it was a parasite feeding on the rebel leaders' collective uncertainty.

The air was heavy with it.

And they knew from experience that fear could breed betrayal. Fear of the enemy or fear of each other.

"Something's wrong," Danny murmured, his voice barely louder than the drip of condensation down the stone walls. But in that silence, his words hit like a thunderclap. "Our last three raids... ambushed. We lost a dozen fighters." His fingers curled into fists, the skin over his knuckles stretched tight. "It's like they knew we were coming."

The murmurs that followed were laced with dread. Eyes darted from shadow to shadow, looking for an enemy that wore the face of a friend.

Tommy's gaze sharpened as he studied their expressions, one by one.

Searching for the Judas in their midst.

"Which means," Tommy said, his voice a blade slicing through the tension, "we have a traitor."

The single bulb hanging overhead flickered, its dying light casting jagged shadows that twisted like writhing serpents along the cracked stone walls.

"It's impossible to know that for sure." Eli blurted out, too quickly, too loudly. His voice cracked, the tremor betraying him. He shrank back, his body pressing against the cold, unforgiving wall as if he could disappear into the cracks that spider-webbed through the ancient stone.

"Is it?" Tommy's tone was colder than the grave, his piercing stare pinning Eli like an insect on a needle. "Because unless you've got another explanation, I'd say it's the only thing that makes sense."

Silence fell, thick and suffocating.

The weight of suspicion settled on them all, pressing down like the earth above their heads.

Danny's voice, rough with barely restrained fury, shattered the stillness. "Brothers and sisters," he said, his tone carrying both authority and desperation, "we're fighting for our survival. Our freedom. We can't let suspicion tear us apart."

"Then what do you suggest we do?" a woman asked, her voice laced with the strain of sleepless nights and relentless fear.

"Trust is a luxury we can't afford anymore," Tommy said grimly. "From now on, the leadership keeps mission plans locked down until the last possible moment. No loose ends. No unnecessary risks. And we watch. Closely. The traitor will slip up." His jaw clenched as his gaze swept over them. "They always do."

The group dispersed, but the silence that followed wasn't relief — it was a funeral march.

As the rebels returned to their duties, their movements were jerky, eyes flickering constantly to the shadows. The paranoia thickened, twisting the air tighter around them like a noose. The tunnels felt more like a cage with every step they took.

Tommy and Danny retreated to the strategy chamber, where the weight of their responsibilities pressed down like a tombstone. The walls, lined with maps streaked by veins of red string, bore the bleeding lifeblood of the rebellion — arteries choked with the constant threat of betrayal.

Tommy leaned over the table, his fingers tracing potential escape routes across the worn map, but even his steady hand betrayed him now. A slight tremor echoed through his fingertips — a crack in the unyielding façade he had worn since childhood.

"We need a plan," he murmured, his voice barely louder than the groan of the ancient timbers that framed the bunker's fragile sanctuary.

"We'll find the rat," Danny said, but the weight in his tone made the promise feel hollow. Exhaustion had dulled his usual fire, replacing it with the weariness of a soldier who had seen too much and lost too many. His voice was strained, cracked at the edges like the brittle walls that confined them. "And when we do..."

"Let's just keep everyone alive until then," Tommy cut him off, his words landing like a death knell, grim and hollow.

It was a tall order. They both knew it.

The cost of betrayal had already been measured in blood and sacrifice.

As they stood there, shoulder to shoulder, the oppressive silence settled around them like a shroud. The weight of their world, of the rebellion teetering on the edge of collapse, pressed down harder than the stone above their heads.

It was suffocating.

The rebellion was not just a fight. It was a living thing, fed by sacrifice and starved by betrayal. And now, that lifeblood was running thin — too thin.

They didn't speak of it, but both felt the rot of uncertainty clawing at the foundation of their resolve. How had their mother carried this weight for so long?

Sage Steel — The Wraith — had not only raised them in the ashes of a fallen world but forged them into weapons of the rebellion while leading the resistance against the Crimson Empire. She had molded them from the bones of a shattered nation, giving them steel in their spines and fire in their veins.

And yet, she had borne that burden alone. For ten years.

A decade.

Tommy could still hear her voice from those early days — soft but unyielding — whispering survival strategies as she stitched up his wounds. He could still feel the fierce grip of her hand on his shoulder the first time he held a gun, steadying him when the weight felt too heavy.

And now she was gone.

The thought of their mother, bound and broken in Pilatus's grasp, was a wound neither of them could bear to touch. The possibility of her permanent loss loomed over them, a specter of pain too immense to acknowledge out loud. Even between them.

They didn't speak her name, not when the ache was this raw.

But the ghost of her sacrifice lingered in the silence — a heavy presence that wrapped around their hearts and refused to let go.

They stood side by side, two sons of Sage Steel, two sons of The Wraith — burdened with a legacy they could feel cracking beneath their feet.

A legacy that was bleeding out.

And in that terrible, suffocating silence, both brothers mutely acknowledged the same cold, terrifying truth:

If they didn't uncover the traitor soon, the rebellion would die — strangled in the dark before it ever saw the light.

An attentive student of his mother's, Danny excelled at navigating the darknet. The hum of the computers in the rebel communication center was a constant companion to his vigilance, but tonight, it felt like a heavy mask over the grim task at hand.

Danny's fingers danced across the keyboard, his eyes narrowed in fierce concentration as encrypted messages flickered across the screen. The ghostly glow of the monitors illuminated his face, casting shadows that stretched long and thin across the concrete walls of the rebel communication center.

He was a natural at this — a skill honed from long nights spent under Sage's tutelage, learning how to navigate the information pathways of the darknet. It was one of the few things that he was better than his older brother at. But tonight, the familiar rhythm of his fingers felt heavy, deliberate, as if the air itself was too thick to breathe, let alone move in.

Beside him, Tommy stood silent, a statue of cold resolve. His green eyes, reflected the shifting light of the screens, but the emotion behind them was unreadable. His fists clenched at his sides, the only sign a storm brewed barely contained beneath a thin veneer of control.

"Got something," Danny murmured, the words barely audible over the low hum of the machines. Tension sharpened his voice as an anomalous string of data caught his eye — a thread out of place in the tapestry of encrypted messages sent by the hacktivists.

"Show me," Tommy said, his tone so low it barely carried past the thrum of the hardware.

Danny clicked through the activity logs, his pulse quickening with each movement. The silence in the room wrapped around them like a noose.

Then the video appeared — a grainy, black-and-white feed from one of their newer hidden perimeter cameras that only they and their darknet friends knew about.

A figure moved through the trees.

"Come on," Danny muttered, zooming in, his eyes narrowing.

The figure emerged from the shadows, and both brothers leaned in as the screen revealed a familiar face.

Eli.

The man they had known for years — a man they trusted. The same man who had stood beside them through blood and fire, who had sworn loyalty to the rebellion and to their mother.

But there he was, standing in the woods under the cover of darkness, taking a package from a figure that did not belong in this world.

The video feed shifted to another angle, and the brothers' worst fears were confirmed.

A vampire.

The creature stood just outside the range of the floodlights, but its presence was unmistakable on camera, a place they couldn't hide their true nature; its fangs glinted, and its eyes glowed red with unnatural hunger. The sight of it, so close to their northern base, sent a chill rippling down their spines.

"Jesus Christ..." Tommy whispered, his voice tight.

A sick feeling twisted in Danny's gut.

"Dammit, Eli..." Tommy's jaw clenched, his cheek twitching. His knuckles whitened as his fists curled tighter.

"We confront him," Danny growled low, his usual composure cracking under the weight of rage as the heat of betrayal scorched through his veins.

"Now."

They found Eli in a secluded part of the base working on the air filtration system, where the mountain's chill seeped through the walls like the air in an underground crypt; heavy with damp, the scent of earth and stone wrapped around them like a shroud.

The dim glow of a single lantern flickered, casting jagged shadows across the tunnel's walls as they approached.

Eli looked up, his face bathed in half-light.

"Tommy... Danny..." His voice cracked, brittle and thin. "How's it going? What's up?"

The words hung in the air like a desperate prayer, but the tremor in his voice betrayed him. His eyes wouldn't meet theirs.

"Cut the crap, Eli," Danny snapped, his voice edged with cold fury. "We know."

Eli's eyes flicked between them, his posture defensive yet crumbling by the second.

"Know what?" His attempt at feigned ignorance was pathetic and limp, a dead thing that didn't even twitch.

Tommy stepped forward, the weight of judgment in his eyes. He raised his phone, the video playing in muted silence. The grainy footage cast a damning glow onto Eli's face, every flicker of light exposing the truth.

"We saw you," Tommy said, his voice as cold as a grave. "With one of them."

"Why?" Danny demanded.

Eli's shoulders slumped. His head bowed as if the weight of his sins had finally broken him. The light from the phone cast jagged shadows across his features, making him look hollow — already a dead man.

"I... I had no choice..." His voice barely carried over the stillness that followed.

"Choices always exist, Eli," Tommy replied, his tone like winter steel — cold, sharp, and merciless.

Eli's gaze lifted, desperation bleeding into his eyes. "They threatened my family!" he choked out, tears brimming and spilling down his face. "Please ... they said they'd take them ... turn them ... my daughter's sick ... They are the only ones who have the medicine! I didn't know what else to do!"

The silence that followed was absolute.

Tommy's expression remained unreadable, but Danny's blue eyes darkened with something dangerous.

"You think that makes a difference? They threaten everyone's family! They took our mother, and we didn't turn traitor to get her back! Your action have put the whole rebellion at risk," Danny said softly, his voice a low growl that barely restrained the murderous fury beneath. "How many have we lost because of you?"

"Too many," Tommy murmured, his gaze distant — as if counting the names etched into his soul.

Eli crumpled to his knees, the weight of his betrayal crashing down upon him. The ragged sobs that shook his body were the sounds of a man who knew there was no forgiveness left to give.

"I'm so sorry..." he whispered.

But sorry could not resurrect the dead.

"No." Tommy's voice was quiet. Deadly quiet.

"But you will be."

For a heartbeat, no one moved.

Then, like a wild animal sensing death, Eli bolted. His body surged forward in a desperate bid for escape, a last-ditch effort to outrun the inevitable.

"Don't," Tommy growled, but it was too late.

Eli sprinted through the tunnels like a man possessed, his footsteps echoing like a death knell against the stone walls.

But no one outran judgment.

A sharp crack echoed through the tunnels, followed by the dull thud of Eli's body hitting the cold ground. The rifle butt had connected with brutal efficiency.

Tommy and Danny emerged from the tunnel like reapers stepping from the shadows, their eyes trained on the crumpled figure at their feet. A thin runnel of blood oozed from the back of Eli's head, trailing along the cracked stone, seeping into the earth like a sacrificial offering.

"Thanks, Cherry," Danny muttered, his voice devoid of warmth as he glanced at the woman standing over Eli, her rifle still in her hands.

"Anytime, Steel." Cherry smirked, but there was no humor in it — only a predator's satisfaction. "Let's get this fucking traitor where he belongs."

They dragged Eli through the dim corridors, his limp body a weight of betrayal that scraped against the stone floor. His ragged breaths echoed around them, mixing with the distant hum of activity from the rebel base.

The rebels who saw them pass turned away, their eyes filled with silent accusations and barely concealed hatred. None spoke. They all knew. Their Judas had been found, and there was no redemption left to offer.

The chamber where they threw Eli was a cold void of stone and darkness. The air hung thick, as if the walls themselves remembered every drop of blood spilled here. Only a single metal chair occupied the center, its frame bolted to the ground, arms and legs fitted with heavy cuffs stained with rust and bloody memories.

Eli hit the floor with a grunt, his body curling inward like a dying insect, gasping for breath. The faint coppery scent of his own blood filled his nostrils, mingling with the stench of fear and regret.

"On the chair." Tommy's voice was devoid of mercy.

Cherry yanked Eli up by the collar, her grip unrelenting as she forced him into the seat. The cuffs clamped down with a chilling finality, the echo of metal-on-metal reverberating through the chamber like the tolling of a bell.

Tommy and Danny stood before him, their faces carved from stone. The sons of Sage Steel — soldiers shaped by war, betrayal, and loss. But beneath the steel of their exterior, something darker stirred — a hunger for answers, a thirst for justice that burned hotter than phosphate.

"Tell us everything," Tommy said, his tone calm, but calm like the stillness before a tornado. He circled the chair slowly, his footsteps reverberating off the walls, echoing like a countdown.

Eli's head lolled forward, his breaths shallow and uneven.

"Please ..." he rasped, his voice barely above a whisper. "My family ... I had no choice ..."

Tommy's fist shot out like a snake striking. His knuckles connected with Eli's jaw, sending a spray of blood and spit across the whitewashed wall.

"You know how this works, Eli. Tell us everything," Tommy demanded, his voice resonating through the room, "or your family will join you in paying the price."

Cherry, standing behind Eli, wrenched his head back by the hair so his bloodied face was tilted toward the brothers.

Eli's wide eyes, filled with terror and exhaustion, darted between the brothers. His lips quivered as he swallowed back the bitter taste of inevitability. He knew there was no escape; the truth would come out, one way or another.

And he knew the brothers wouldn't touch his family, unless he gave them reason too.

They were honorable that way, like their mother; a woman he had known since before the fangers revealed themselves.

They would not lay his sins on his wife and children.

Unless he lied.

Tommy and Danny stood over him, their faces grim masks of determination.

With each passing second, the air felt heavier. The weight of his betrayal crushed his soul.

"I ... they came to me," Eli stammered, his voice cracking. "When I was in town, getting supplies. I didn't go to them."

Tommy's jaw clenched, but he said nothing.

"They knew about my daughter's illness," Eli whispered, his voice thick with desperation. "They promised medicine ... safety. Said they'd keep her alive if I cooperated." His gaze dropped to the floor, as if the weight of his words crushed him.

"They threatened to turn them," he choked, his body trembling like a man standing on the edge of an abyss. "My wife ... my little ones ..."

"Promises from vampires are poison," Danny interrupted, his fists clenching at his sides. "And you fucking drank it."

Eli's tears spilled over, streaking down his bloodied face. "They made good on their promises. They didn't touch them. Got my daughter the medicine ... besides, I had no choice!" he sobbed, the words barely audible.

"Choices always exist, Eli," Tommy murmured, his voice dripping with cold finality. "You chose wrong."

"So, your family survived while others died? You could have come to us. Told us they approached you. You could have fought back! Die with honor. Not betray your own kind. Not cower and serve those monsters who have killed so many of us!" Danny spat out, his blue eyes blazing with a deadly fury that belied his youth.

"Enough, Danny," Tommy interceded, though his own heart raced with a cocktail of contempt and sorrow. He kneeled down, bringing his face level with Eli's. "We need details, Eli. Routes, numbers, plans. Anything you gave them. What did you tell them?"

"Everything ..." Eli's voice cracked, and he swallowed hard. "Patrol routes, supply caches, attack strategies. I passed it all along. They have known every move before we make it for months. But I didn't give them the headquarters or anything near D.C." He told them hopefully, as if it would make a difference to what happened to him in the end.

The grim reality of Eli's confession settled over the room and outer hallway like a deathly silence. The vampires' reach extended further than they had feared, their tactics more insidious. Every operation, every life lost — it all bore the stain of this treachery.

"Your cowardice has cost us dearly," Danny said, his gaze fixed on Eli, and betrayal squeezed his chest. His brother's eyes mirrored the regret in his own, both burdened by the realization that their rebellion was filled with vulnerabilities, and this could cause the death of many others.

"Did they say what they're planning? Anything about their next move?" Tommy pressed, each word sharpened by urgency.

Eli hesitated, then nodded pathetically. "An assault ... on the northern front. They're massing forces larger than we've ever seen."

Tommy and Danny exchanged a look. The revelation was a double-edged sword — actionable intelligence, but at what cost?

"Is there more?" Danny demanded, a vein throbbing in his temple.

Tommy held up a hand, silencing his brother before he could explode.

He turned back to Eli, his gaze piercing into his soul. "Your family will not suffer for your mistakes," Tommy promised, his voice a low growl, "but you must give us something more we can use. Something that will prevent more needless human death!"

Danny paced behind Tommy like a caged lion, trying to dispel some of his fury.

Eli cringed, a fresh wave of guilt washing over his features. His eyes, rimmed red with fear and fatigue, lifted to meet Tommy's. "My contact mentioned ..." His voice broke, the words tumbling out in a rush of desperation, "The location ... where they're holding S age."

Danny's world stopped.

"Our mother?" The words barely escaped his lips, but the fury behind them made the air vibrate. "How long have you known that?" He snarled, and his brother gripped him hard around the chest, grounding him before he exploded.

"Where?" Tommy's voice was ice, but his eyes burned with something primal.

"An underground cell ... beneath the Cathedral," Eli confessed, his gaze dropping to the cold floor like a sinner before the judgment seat. "They've kept her in a cell in the cathedral's basement ... she's either there or in Pilatus's throne room. They never allow her outside. She's alive but ..."

"Go on," Tommy urged, his voice barely above a whisper.

"They use her to write their history books," Eli choked out. "And when she's finished, they plan to execute her for all to see. She's gonna be their bait."

Silence filled the chamber. A terrible silence.

Tommy held his brother in place, his body trembling with barely contained rage. The weight of their mother's fate hung heavy in the air, suffocating them both.

Danny's jaw clenched, his hands flexing at his sides, as if itching to rend the world apart.

"We need a plan," Tommy murmured, but the promise in his voice was lethal.

Tommy exchanged a look with Danny; their bond as brothers — as soldiers born from rebellion — stronger than steel.

They stepped out of the chamber into the dim torchlight of the tunnels, where the whispers of the rebellion stirred like the rustling of dead leaves.

"Tommy," Danny cautioned, his voice barely above a whisper, but the warning in it was clear. "This could be a trap."

Their mother, the very heart of their rebellion, was within reach — yet their enemy still had her gripped in their talons. An enemy that they and the others had already retreated from once on their mother's orders.

Tommy's jaw clenched, but he didn't hesitate.

"I know," he replied. "But it's Mom."

A TRAITOR'S REWARD

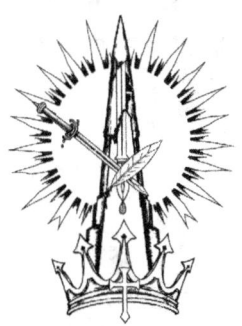

THE METALLIC CHILL OF the chair gnawed through Eli's clothes, a merciless contrast to the warm, sluggish trickle of blood meandering down his temple. The iron scent mingled with the damp air, painting the small chamber with the aroma of treachery. The blood was fresh — a crimson signature of his betrayal, signing away lives that couldn't be reclaimed.

His erstwhile comrades stood before him, no longer brothers in arms but executioners-in-waiting.

Tommy's jaw clenched, his teeth grinding like millstones, the weight of Eli's confession echoing in his mind like a funeral bell. Shadows pooled beneath his eyes, dark with sleepless nights and burdened resolve. His knuckles whitened as his fingers curled into fists at his sides, but his voice, when it came, was cold and controlled. Too controlled.

"Specifically where?" Tommy's demand sliced through the suffo-cating silence, sharp and unforgiving — a scalpel poised to carve the truth from Eli's lips.

Eli swallowed hard, his throat dry as dust. "An underground cell," he rasped, each word trembling under the weight of impend-ing doom. "Beneath the eastside cathedral spire. That's where they are holding Sage. You can get to the basement level... through the underground parking garage."

The mention of their mother — The Wraith, the beating heart of the rebellion — dangled before them like a crucifix in the hands of a dying martyr. Hope.

A spark ignited in Tommy's eyes, but it wasn't warmth. It was something colder, sharper — the glint of vengeance restrained by purpose.

Danny, prowling like a restless predator, froze mid-pace, his fists clenched tight at his sides. His breath hissed between gritted teeth as his body vibrated with unspent rage. His blue eyes, once filled with boyish mischief, now burned with something feral.

"You swear?" Danny's voice was a low growl, the sound of a wolf circling its prey. "You're not playing us? You know what happens to your family if you are."

The threat hung heavy in the air, a blade suspended by a fraying thread.

Eli's head bobbed like a puppet on frayed strings. "Check my intel," he whispered, desperation thickening his voice. "Check with the hacktivists. You'll see it's solid." His words tumbled out in a frantic rush, his eyes darting between them like a man drowning, searching for a lifeline.

"My contact complained enough about the extra patrols Pilatus had stationed in that part of the cathedral." Eli's breath hitched, his throat convulsing with dread. "He didn't know who she really was — just that Pilatus called her his 'precious writer pet.' Extra guards. Inside and out. But with manpower stretched thin... they only reinforce that one side. The hackers... they should see the increased activity through the D.C. CCTV."

Tommy's eyes narrowed, dissecting every word. Lies would be sniffed out like a rotting corpse.

And Tommy would not suffer lies.

An unspoken exchange passed between the brothers — a dialogue carved from years of survival and trust in a world where trust was a liability. Danny's brow furrowed, suspicion coiling around him like smoke, while Tommy's expression remained carved from stone, unreadable yet deadly.

But they both felt it.

The weight of their situation pressed down, heavy as the earth that would bury them all if they failed. Eli's confession was a thread pulled from the fragile lace of their rebellion. One wrong move and everything — everyone — would unravel.

A chill seeped into the room, not from the cold stone walls, but from the sense of something far darker closing in.

Tommy's voice was quieter when it came, but no less dangerous.

"If this is a trap, Eli..." He didn't finish the sentence. He didn't have to.

The threat was a promise etched in the blood of Eli's family.

Eli's head dipped, eyes squeezing shut as the enormity of his sin bore down on him. "I swear, that's all I know."

And somewhere in the back of his mind, as he faced the judgment of the boys he watched grow up, Eli wondered if Judas had felt the same icy knot of dread after the silver touched his hands.

"Alright." Tommy's voice was low but resolute, a whisper of thunder that rumbled just beneath the surface. His eyes, sharp as obsidian, scanned the darknet reports from his mother's contacts, his expression hardening with grim resolve. The flickering glow of the monitors cast jagged shadows across his face, carving deep lines of exhaustion that even his youth couldn't smooth away.

"We move fast," he murmured, as if speaking the words aloud would bend fate to his will. "Before Pilatus realizes we're onto him."

Maps sprawled across the table like sacrificial offerings, veins of red string connecting cities, outposts, and danger zones. Maps of war, drawn now in the blood of the fallen. Fluorescent lights hummed overhead, sterile and cold, but they could not dispel the oppressive weight that thickened the air.

Gunmetal and old paper mingled with the scent of sweat and fear. Each rebel captain crowded around the table, their faces etched with battle-hardened resolve — but behind their eyes lurked a shadow of unease. Fear. Not of death. Of failure. For the future. And never for themselves; only for those that would be left behind.

"We can't ignore this chance," Tommy declared, his finger tracing a jagged route on the map. His touch was light, but the gravity in his tone was heavy, like the stone door to a dark tomb. "It's time to hit them where it hurts."

A scarred veteran, his face a roadmap of past battles, nodded gravely. His voice, barely a whisper, carried the weight of a soldier who had seen too many comrades buried. "Agreed."

But not everyone was convinced.

"Wait." Danny's voice sliced through the tension, his brow furrowed with suspicion. His eyes, burned with doubt. "We need to consider something. What if this is a trap?" His gaze swept the room, the unspoken fears reflected at him in the eyes of those gathered.

"Pilatus isn't known for mercy or mistakes. And why didn't Mom send her location herself? We've been getting her messages through the darknet for months..."

The words hung heavy, but in them was a seed of uncertainty ready to take root.

Tommy's jaw clenched, but his voice was steady. "Maybe she didn't know." His gaze didn't waver as he met Danny's eyes. "Maybe they took her blindfolded. Or maybe..." His voice dropped to a whisper, filled with a pain he wouldn't speak aloud, "Maybe she didn't want anyone else dying over her."

The memory of that night six months ago pressed in like a phantom, Sage's last order echoing through the halls of their minds.

"Retreat. Now."

Her voice had been diamond-hard, unyielding, even as the vampires closed in. She had surrendered herself to Pilatus to save them. And they had obeyed — but not without a cost.

Tommy's throat tightened, but he pushed the pain down where it couldn't show. "Every mission has its risks," he said softly, his voice barely above the rustle of paper. Then armor coated his words. "But think of the reward."

He leaned forward, his hands braced against the table, his eyes piercing into the souls of those around him.

"Rescuing Sage. Rescuing The Wraith. Striking at the heart of Pilatus himself. Pilatus has obsessed over her since the beginning, since before they took over the governments. We owe it to her." His voice dropped, raw with emotion. "To everyone we've lost."

The silence that followed was not empty — it was pregnant with purpose. A quiet, burning resolve that spread through the room like wildfire.

A wave of agreement rippled through the rebels, their fear momentarily drowned out by the roar of determination. They had no choice. This was not just a rescue mission. It was retribution.

"But what about the northern base?" Cherry's voice, calm but edged with concern, broke through the murmur of assent. Her dark eyes met Tommy's, her question heavy with implications.

Tommy didn't hesitate. "That's yours, Cherry."

Her brows lifted, but her expression was all business.

"Get your team together. We'll send a message directing evacuation of families and non-combatants." His tone was grim, a general issuing orders before a war that could end them all.

"We'll take a small rescue team to the cathedral — no more than half a dozen. We go in and out... fast."

"The rest are yours." His eyes locked on Cherry's, the unspoken command etched in the space between them. "Take the reinforcements to the north ... and kill those fuckers."

Cherry's lips curled into a dangerous smile. "Consider it done."

Tommy's voice was iron wrapped in velvet when he spoke again. "Let's gather the teams. We move out tomorrow at nightfall."

And somewhere beyond the stone walls, the night stirred, eager for blood.

The moon hung low and sickly, its pale light strangled by the dense canopy of twisted branches above. Silver fingers struggled to pierce through the veil of night, casting fractured beams that barely illuminated the grim stage below. The air was thick, damp with the scent of moss and decay — as if the forest itself recoiled from the act about to unfold.

A monument to betrayal had been erected in the clearing. The gallows stood like a skeletal sentinel, its wooden frame rough-hewn and splintered, as though hastily carved by hands eager to deliver judgment. The rope, thick and coarse, swung lazily in the night breeze, whispering promises of finality to the man who stood before it

Eli stumbled forward, his hands bound tightly behind him, wrists already raw and bleeding from his futile struggles. The two rebels who escorted him — faces carved from stone and hearts hardened by war — marched him toward his fate with the indifferent precision of executioners.

The noose dangled before him like a serpent, a loop of judgment that promised only one outcome. And Eli's sin was beyond forgiveness.

His eyes, once alight with deceit and false loyalty, were now dull and glassy, reflecting the inevitability of what was to come. The act of betrayal had long since extinguished the original, leaving only a hollow shell of the man they had once trusted.

Tommy and Danny stood at the forefront of the gathered rebels, their faces etched with lines too deep for men so young. Brothers by blood, leaders by necessity, executioners by consequence.

Tommy's jaw was clenched so tight it felt as if his teeth might crack, but he said nothing. His green eyes — mirrors of Sage's strength — betrayed no emotion, but his fists curled at his sides as if trying to crush the doubt that gnawed at the edges of his resolve.

Betrayal left wounds deeper than any blade.

Danny, pacing like a predator just out of reach, radiated barely contained fury. His movements were restless, his fingers flexing with the desire to strike. But it was not his hand that would deliver justice tonight.

"Specifically where?" Tommy's question echoed in Eli's ears long after it was spoken. And now, with the answers given, and the confession extracted, there was nothing left but judgment.

Eli's knees buckled as he was positioned beneath the gallows, his breathing shallow, a pitiful whisper against the stillness of the forest. The noose was lowered, its shadow stretching like an omen across the damp earth, a grim reminder that some sins demand more than absolution.

The gathered rebels formed a silent congregation, their faces masked by darkness and grief.

This was no joyous execution. No triumph of crimes discovered.

This was a crucifixion of trust.

Eli's eyes lifted, seeking mercy where there was none.

"Please..." His voice was a cracked whisper, barely audible. But he knew that any mercy had died long ago the moment innocent blood had been spilled.

Tommy met his gaze, his expression unreadable. "Judas took thirty pieces of silver," he murmured, his words a chilling benediction. "You took the blood of your brothers."

Eli flinched, tears pooling in his eyes as he glanced toward the sky — but even Heaven had turned its back.

No more words. Only silence.

Tommy's boot slammed against the wooden platform with merciless force.

The floor dropped away.

Eli's body plummeted, not far enough to break his neck, though the sudden jerk of the rope snapping his head back did so with a sickening crack. His limbs convulsed violently, the crude dance of death painting a morbid picture of agony. His legs kicked frantically, boots scuffing the edge of the crude scaffold as though seeking a toehold for a salvation that would never come.

Veins bulged grotesquely in his neck, engorged and pulsing with the last, futile struggles of life. The noose bit deeper, grinding against flesh, the fibers tearing through skin and muscle.

His face turned a sickening shade of purple, veins spidering beneath the surface as blood pooled where it could no longer flow. His tongue, swollen and useless, protruded grotesquely between his lips, contorting his face into a hideous mask of pain. His wide, bulging eyes reflected raw terror and regret, capturing the moment he truly understood the finality of his betrayal.

Guttural grunts and strangled gurgles escaped his throat, each sound a grotesque note of suffering. His windpipe constricted, crushed beneath the relentless embrace of the noose, and with every fleeting second, his struggles grew weaker — his defiance fading into the encroaching void.

Bones ground together as his body jerked and spasmed, the dying embers of resistance flickering one last time before surrendering to the dark. The tension in the rope was merciless, unyielding, until finally...

Stillness.

The echo of death lingered in the air. Eli's lifeless body hung limp, the noose swaying gently, as if cradling the traitor's corpse in a perverse lullaby. A pendulum marking the passage of justice.

The only sound was the rhythmic creak of the rope, a grim reminder that mercy had no place in this world.

Tommy's fists clenched tighter, his knuckles white against the weight of what they had just done. Each twitch of Eli's legs had been an accusation, a reminder that justice carried a price; for both the dead and the living.

But betrayal was a cancer to the entire human race, and they had to cut it out.

Inside Eli's fading mind, where terror clashed with regret, a single tear fought its way free. A lone drop of sorrow, not for himself, but for the shattered world he had helped damn. A tear for the woman who had inspired hope — and whose sons had now been forced to extinguish another life in her name.

Danny stood rigid, his gaze locked on the lifeless body swaying above the earth. His anger had not burned away the emptiness left behind. He had expected vengeance to be satisfying, but all he felt was the chilling hollowness that came with taking a life — even one so undeserving.

The gathered rebels stood in silence, their faces unreadable masks. Relief, sorrow, and grim satisfaction tangled in their hearts, but none spoke.

This was war. And in war, mercy was weakness.

"Let this be a warning." Tommy's voice, when it finally came, was like the crack of a whip through the cold air. "We are at war, and all blood-traitors will suffer the same fate."

The rebels bowed their heads. Not in prayer — for God had long since abandoned this land — but in grim acknowledgment of the cost of survival.

As the last echoes of justice faded into the forest, the moon turned away, hiding its light from the horrors man was forced to commit in the name of freedom.

Eli's body hung as a silent warning. A testament to the unrelenting brutality of war and the reward for betrayal.

And as Tommy and Danny turned away, they carried the weight of another soul added to their ledger.

A soul weighed down by thirty pieces of blood.

The gallows still whispered in their ears. The creak of rope, the last spasms of a traitor's body, and the suffocating stillness that followed — echoes that refused to be silenced, no matter how far they walked from the place where Eli had paid the price for his sins.

But there was no time for lingering ghosts.

Tommy and Danny led the way back into the heart of their rebellion, their boots kicking up dust that settled over the memories of the condemned. The strategy room, carved deep into the mountain's embrace, awaited them like a tomb filled with the artifacts of a dying cause.

Maps, blueprints, and battle plans lay strewn across the scarred wooden table, fluttering slightly in the draft that wormed through the stone cracks. The lanterns hanging from the ceiling flickered with restless energy, their weak flames casting erratic shadows that danced like harbingers of doom on the cold stone walls. Every flicker seemed to breathe life into the whispered warnings of those who had died before — silent voices urging caution, reminding them of the cost of failure.

Tommy stood at the table's head, his broad shoulders squared with the burden of command. His green eyes scanned the chaos before him with a steely focus. But beneath that mask of control, the weight of what was to come pressed down on him like a stone slab. Every map, every line drawn across the parchment, was etched in blood — the blood of those who had fought and died to get them this far.

"Here." Tommy's voice cut through the tension, low and steady, but the undertone of urgency was impossible to miss. His finger traced a jagged route across the blueprint of the cathedral's vaults — a path carved through shadows and secrets. "This is where they're holding her."

The room seemed to shrink around them. The walls, once a haven for strategy and planning, now felt suffocating — a silent reminder that the fate of their rebellion rested on this one mission.

"We'll hit the east entrance," Tommy murmured, his gaze narrowing as he traced their intended path through a labyrinth of catacombs and underground corridors. "Through the old parking structure. Less visibility. Fewer patrols." His jaw clenched. "If Eli's intel holds."

Eli's ghost hung in the air, a lingering specter of betrayal.

Danny stood beside him, his face shadowed by the dim glow of the lanterns. The flickering light caught the hard planes of his jaw, highlighting the grim determination that had settled into his features. But his fingers drummed lightly on the edge of the table — a habit he hadn't shaken since childhood. A tell that revealed the storm raging beneath his composed exterior.

"I'll lead the front assault." Danny's voice was steady, but there was a hunger in it — a hunger for vengeance, for redemption. "It's the riskiest route, but I know the streets of D.C. better than anyone." His finger hovered over the map, tracing an alternate route that led through the ruins of old Washington. "I can guide us through the back alleys and collapsed tunnels."

Tommy's gaze met his brother's, the weight of unspoken understanding passing between them. This wasn't just about strategy. This was personal. "You're sure?"

"I'm sure." Danny's voice left no room for argument. The fire in his blue eyes burned too brightly for Tommy to extinguish. He was ready to do whatever it took — even if it meant facing death head-on.

One by one, the rebels around the table claimed their roles, each volunteer stepping into the unfolding narrative like pieces moving on a chessboard.

Cherry, her expression hardened by the weight of command, claimed the northern defense. "I'll handle the evacuation of the northern base," she said, her voice cool but edged with steel. "We'll pull out the families and torch the supplies before the bloodsuckers get their hands on anything useful."

Tommy gave a curt nod. "Good. Make them regret ever stepping foot on our soil."

The others followed suit, claiming their parts in the intricate ballet of war. Each understood the stakes — recognizing that unity was their greatest weapon and that sacrifice might be demanded of them before all was done. They weren't just planning an assault. They were preparing to walk into the jaws of death.

Tommy straightened, his hands bracing against the edge of the table as he surveyed the surrounding faces. Every set of eyes reflected the same grim resolve that burned in his chest.

"Everyone get some sleep." The words felt hollow, but there was no room for sentiment now. "Both teams leave at dusk. And remember — timing is everything."

His gaze locked onto Danny's, then moved across the room, meeting the eyes of every rebel gathered. "If we miss our window, Sage dies. And if she dies..." Tommy's voice dropped to a whisper, but the weight behind it was crushing. "...then we all die."

The silence that followed was heavier than any speech could have been. A silence that carried the weight of understanding, the cold kiss of mortality pressing against their throats.

As they dispersed to prepare — to gather their weapons, their thoughts, and their courage — the strategy room grew colder.

The lanterns flickered, casting distorted shadows that twisted and writhed across the walls like vengeful spirits. Whispers of martyrs filled the room, voices of the fallen echoing from the darkness.

They whispered of sacrifice. Of hope.

And of blood.

Tommy lingered, his fingertips brushing against the map one last time. The route to the cathedral was etched into his mind, but the path forward was shrouded in uncertainty. His heart pounded with the weight of every life that hung in the balance.

"Please," he murmured, a whispered prayer to the mother who had taught him how to survive in a world gone mad. "Hold on."

As the room emptied and the last echoes of footsteps faded, the oppressive silence pressed down on him once more.

The hours ahead would either see them as liberators or send them to join the countless martyrs whose whispers already seemed to fill the air.

And if they failed...

Sage Steel's final chapter would be written in blood.

On one of the grand cathedral's shadowed balconies, Pilatus paced. The stone beneath his feet was cold and unyielding, mirroring the unease that had taken root in his heart. His keen ears picked up the subtle shift in tone amongst his subjects, whispers that were not of reverence but of doubt.

Sage's writings, spread like a virus through FaceFang, had done their work well, seeding discord among the once unwaveringly loyal vampires.

"More guards," he barked at a nearby attendant, who bowed hastily before scurrying away. "And double the surveillance on all communication channels." His voice echoed off the vaulted ceilings, betraying the brittleness of his paranoia.

The walls inside seemed to listen, festooned with ancient tapestries from Rome that bore witness to centuries of dominance of the Roman Empire. Now they seemed to look upon the Crimson Empire and its Blood Monarch as insurrection threatened them from within and without.

Pilatus' grip tightened around the iron balcony railing, his knuckles blanching, as he looked out over the streets of the former human capital, a silent vow to crush any uprising before it could draw breath.

Dusk settled over the rebel base, painting the sky in bruised shades of crimson and gold. The air hummed with tension as weapons were checked and rechecked, magazines loaded with meticulous care. Maps were folded and stashed away, while whispered prayers echoed softly in the corners of the bunker.

Tommy found Danny standing alone near the edge of camp, his silhouette etched against the dying light. His expression was hard, carved from the same iron resolve that had kept them alive all these years.

"We knew it would come to this," Tommy murmured, stepping beside his brother, their shoulders nearly touching.

Danny's jaw clenched, but his voice was steady. "Risking everything for one life... She wouldn't want that." His gaze stayed fixed on the horizon. "But she's more than just our mother, Tommy. She's the reason they haven't broken us."

Tommy nodded, his hand clapping lightly on Danny's back. "Then let's make sure she doesn't pay the price for our failure."

Their eyes met, a silent vow passing between them. Whatever came next, they would face it together. Like always.

Before another word could be spoken, a sudden shift in the air announced Cherry's arrival.

"Steel." Her voice was low, but her intent was anything but subtle.

Danny lacked time to react before Cherry closed the distance, her hands gripping his shirt as if anchoring herself to him. Her lips crashed into his, the kiss fierce and unrelenting. Their bodies molded together, a collision of heat and desperation that had simmered too long beneath the surface. Her grip around him tightened, pulling him deeper into the embrace as if she sought to merge their very beings into one. Their breaths mingled in the space between them; each exhale was a testament to the fiery passion that burned within.

Tommy, wide-eyed, stood frozen as Cherry pulled back, her breath mingling with Danny's in the fading light. A smirk tugged at her lips as she patted his ass with a teasing slap.

"You keep that warm for me, Steel," she murmured, her voice a sultry promise. "Until I get back."

Danny, grinning like an idiot, called after her as she walked rapidly away. "Right back at you!"

Tommy shook his head, his lips twitching. "Isn't she ... closer to Mom's age than yours?"

Danny's grin only widened. "Jealous?"

Tommy's fist connected with Danny's arm, eliciting a dramatic "Ow!" from his younger brother.

"I'm telling Mom," Tommy deadpanned, already walking away.

"Oh, come on!" Danny groaned, chasing after him. "Don't do me like that, bro!"

Their banter faded as they rejoined the others, but the shift was tangible. The moment of levity vanished, replaced by a cold, lethal resolve that settled over the rebels like a second skin.

Vehicles rumbled to life, engines growling softly in the encroaching dark. Every rebel was armored not just with weapons, but with the grim determination of those who had already buried too many friends.

As they pulled away from the base, the haunting image of Eli's lifeless body swaying from the gallows in their review mirrors burned into their minds. A chilling reminder of what failure cost.

And as the night swallowed them whole, Tommy and Danny's thoughts were the same —

Rescue Sage. Or die trying.

THE CHAINS OF IMMORTALITY

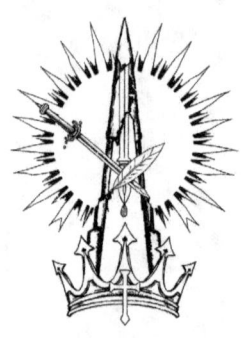

PILATUS LEANED FORWARD, HIS eyes narrowing as the grainy black-and-white image of Sage flickered across the surveillance screen. Her movements, fluid and precise, were a dance of defiance — a silent rebellion that echoed louder than words. The dim glow of the monitor bathed his angular features in a pale, unholy light, casting deep shadows that stressed the centuries of cruelty carved into his face.

Millennia had sharpened his instincts, honed his patience, and sculpted him into a master manipulator. He had adapted to the changing world, bending it to his will while many of his progeny fumbled in the dark, lost in the puzzle of modernity. Technology, once a novelty, extended his power — an invisible hand that allowed him to reach across vast distances and tighten his grip on his domain.

And yet...

The sight of her stirred something ancient, something dangerous. A hunger deeper than the craving for blood, more potent than the lust for domination. It was maddening. She was merely a woman — fragile, fleeting, and breakable — and yet, she refused to yield.

"Remarkable," he murmured, his voice barely above a whisper, the word laced with a twisted reverence.

A cold draft slithered through the chamber, rustling the edges of ancient tapestries that hung like forgotten memories on the stone walls. The scent of aged parchment and the decaying echoes of history filled the air, a familiar balm that usually calmed him. But not tonight. Tonight, the aroma mingled with the iron tang of his own impatience — a bitter taste that curled on his tongue as he watched her pace the confines of her prison.

Sage Steel.

Her name was a curse and a prayer, a thorn that embedded itself deeper with every glance. Her resilience was an affront to his supremacy — a flame that refused to be extinguished. Every deliberate movement, every flick of her wrist or shift of her gaze, defied the very order he had built. And still... he admired her.

Admired her enough to want to break her.

Pilatus's fingers ghosted along the edge of the monitor, the cool plastic casing a stark contrast to the heat simmering within him. His touch was gentle, almost reverent, as though he could feel her through the screen.

But his eyes told a different story — dark, hungry, and brimming with an unholy promise.

She would kneel.

Not because he demanded it. Not because he was Pilatus, the Blood Monarch.

But because she would have no choice.

His soul — what little remained of it — yearned to unravel her, to watch as her strength crumbled under the unbearable weight of

eternity. To strip her bare of her mortal resolve until only submission remained.

"You'll yield," he whispered to the empty room, his voice a
caress of shadow and steel, as if the walls themselves could bear
witness to his oath.

A predator's smile ghosted across his lips.

And when she broke...

He would savor every fractured piece.

The heavy door groaned open, its ancient hinges protesting as
Sage stepped into the chamber. The flickering torchlight danced
along the blood-red carpet, muffling her footsteps but doing
nothing to soften the weight of her presence. The air was thick
— charged with something raw and primal. It was not fear that
hung between them, but a tension so taut that it felt as though
the very stones of the cathedral held their breath.

Pilatus did not rise. He remained seated, his silhouette a carved
monolith upon the throne-like chair, his posture a languid pose.
But his eyes...

His eyes devoured her.

"Sage." Her name rolled off his tongue like a lover's caress, but
there was steel beneath the velvet. "I've been thinking about...
gifts."

Her expression didn't change, but the slightest flicker of wari-
ness rippled in her emerald gaze. "Really?" The word was a
dagger, sharp and pointed, laced with disdain and boredom.

"Immortality." Pilatus's voice was a dark lullaby, each syllable
laced with promise and peril. "The ultimate gift one can bestow."

His eyes tracked her as she moved, each step closer a study in defiance. She stopped just out of his reach, her chin lifted in muted defiance, her posture unyielding despite the gravity of the moment.

"Gift?" Sage's tone was icy, her words a blade that sliced through the illusion of his benevolence. "Or is it a chain, Pilatus? A shackle to bind me to your side as your pet? Your... historian? Trapped in a cage of eternity while you rewrite history to your liking."

Pilatus's lips curled into a bitter smile, but the brief flicker of irritation in his eyes betrayed his frustration. Her words had struck a nerve, scraping against the delicate façade he presented. "You see chains where I offer freedom," he murmured, though the lie dripped like venom from his tongue.

Pilatus's gaze lingered on her, his admiration for her spirit warring with the desire to break it.

"Freedom to be what? Your puppet? Your mouthpiece?" She folded her arms over her breasts, as if to shield to her body. Her posture spoke volumes of her refusal to bend. "To document the slow decay of a world bled dry by your empire?"

Pilatus rose, his movements fluid but predatory, the space between them diminishing with each step. "The world changes every day, Sage," he said softly, his voice a dark promise. "And even we... change with it." His eyes gleamed with something ancient and dangerous, a flicker of vulnerability buried beneath layers of arrogance. "But together..." His voice dropped lower, seductive and insidious. "Ours could be the last empire — one that outlasts the rise and fall of every nation."

"An empire built on fear and blood. Feeding on your kin." Sage's eyes flashed with fury, her words a searing accusation. "That's not living, Pilatus. That's existence — and it's hollow."

For a moment, the air thickened, and the space between them became a battlefield where neither would yield. The tension coiled tighter, the pulse of it reverberating through the chamber like a heartbeat.

Pilatus stepped closer, and Sage instinctively took a step back, her body braced for what might come. But he was relentless, closing the gap with a predator's grace. The exchange left Pilatus momentarily without words, his thoughts swirling like the incense smoke that curled up towards the vaulted ceiling. He stepped closer, the space between them charged with the energy of their confrontation.

"You know, Sage, we vampires don't need humans."

She took another step away from him. "Of course you do! You need us so you can live! To drink our blood! To make more vampires!"

He stepped toward her, closing the distance between them once more. "We can take the nutrient we need through the blood of any mammal. Human beings are singularly unnecessary in obtaining this nutrient, as we can get it from anywhere."

"Liar! If we weren't necessary, you would have wiped us out years ago!" She told him, stepping toward him in her fury, all traces of fear gone, as her green eyes snapped in anger.

"We don't need humans, but that doesn't mean that we don't find humans fascinating. It doesn't mean that we don't lust for them either sexually or to feed upon. Because we do not need humans to live, that doesn't mean that we don't enjoy their company, or even the way they think. Their lives are very short, and because of that, they live with such gusto. That makes them fascinating. And we..." His hand hovered near her face, his fingers brushing the air as if tempted to close the distance. "We were all human once."

Sage stood her ground, her pulse pounding in her ears, but her resolve did not waver. "And that's the tragedy," she said softly, her words like a curse that echoed through the silence. "You forgot what it means to be human."

The heat of her defiance seared him. For a moment, Pilatus's mask slipped, and something raw flickered in his dark gaze — admiration, desire ... rage.

Sage didn't flinch, her rejection clear as she met his gaze. "I'd rather embrace death than be part of your undead dynasty." Pilatus's jaw clenched, the muscles in his face tightening with barely restrained fury. His hand fell to his side, his fingers curling into a fist as the weight of her rejection settled like lead in his chest.

"Such a waste," he murmured, but his tone was colder now, a promise of retribution.

With a flick of his wrist, Victor emerged from the shadows, his presence brought by a silent command.

"Escort her back," Pilatus said, his voice devoid of warmth. "We'll ... continue this conversation another time."

As Sage was led away, her absence left a void that echoed through the chamber, but her defiance lingered like a ghost haunting Pilatus in the hollow stillness.

Alone once more, he turned back to the shadows, but his mind remained ensnared by her. His obsession had deepened, thickening like a poison in his veins.

The game he played was a long one; after all, for him time meant nothing.

And in the end...

She would be his.

Later that evening, Pilatus summoned Sage to his private quarters once more, a ritual that had become as predictable as the moon's rise. The opulent chamber was bathed in the glow of candlelight, its gilded edges and velvet drapes a stark contrast to the shadow that had taken root within its master.

She refused to eat. Again.

Pilatus glanced at the untouched plate, his attention consumed by her words from earlier — words that refused to dissipate, clinging to the edges of his consciousness like a persistent ghost.

"*Unrest in a populace is a poison, Pilatus.*" Her voice echoed in his mind, a whispered refrain that gnawed at the edges of his composure. "*It seeps through the ranks, even among the immortal. They whisper, you know... about your choices, about your leadership.*"

Pilatus stood at the towering window that overlooked the sprawling city below, the flickering lights of the human quarters resembling dying stars in a sky that had forgotten how to dream. His reflection was almost invisible in the glass — a faint distortion, a shadow of what once was. The city had been remade in his image, yet her words echoed through its streets, threading doubt through the very fabric of his empire.

"*Even empires crumble, Pilatus. And time erodes all certainties.*"

A muscle twitched in his jaw, the only outward sign of the turmoil that simmered beneath his polished exterior. He had lived through the fall of Rome, watched kingdoms rot from within, crumbled by whispers and doubt. The seeds of insurrection were always sown in silence, long before the first sword was drawn. And now, those seeds had been planted — by her.

By Sage.

His grip tightened on the goblet in his hand, the cool metal bending slightly beneath his strength. Blood-spiced wine, aged to perfection, painted a crimson line down the side of the goblet, trailing like a wound. He brought it to his lips, the taste of iron mingling with the bitterness of unspoken fears.

"Destiny is not swayed by whispers, my Sage," he had told her, his voice steady, but the words felt hollow now, echoing in the vast emptiness of the chamber. "It is carved by those strong enough to wield power and make the difficult choices."

Yet her gaze had been unwavering, a mirror reflecting his deepest anxieties back at him. She hadn't needed to speak. Her silence had screamed louder than any accusation, her arched brow and tilted head a subtle, devastating challenge.

And he had felt it.

A break.

Small, but present.

For the first time in centuries, doubt whispered in his ear — and it spoke with her voice.

Pilatus inhaled, savoring the cool night air that seeped through the cracks of the ancient stone walls. The scent of rain and decay intertwined, a reminder that even immortality was not immune to rot.

"Immortality is both a gift and a burden," he had confessed to her — a moment of vulnerability he now cursed. "An endless cycle of responsibilities, a constant battle against the sweeping storms of change. I fight to protect the people and the empire through a slow and stable transition through time."

But she had seen through him. Beneath the constructed façade of indomitable power, she had sensed the fatigue, the weight of an eternity spent preserving an empire that refused to remain silent.

"Even empires crumble, Pilatus." Her soft words had been a dagger to his heart. *"And time erodes all certainties."*

Pilatus's eyes darkened as they traced the city's skyline.

His empire would not crumble. He would not allow it.

"Perhaps," he had murmured to her, his voice barely above a whisper.

But in that moment, he had lied — to her, and to himself.

Because he did not intend to rule until the stars burned out.

He would outlast them.

As Sage was escorted back to her cell, Pilatus remained rooted to the spot, his gaze locked onto the empty corridor displayed on the surveillance screen. Her defiance haunted him, lingering in the air like the scent of her skin — an intoxicating mixture of danger and allure.

"Remarkable," he whispered, his voice barely above the rustle of the drapes behind him.

But this...

This was no longer a game of power.

Pilatus's obsession had evolved — from admiration... to possession... to something darker.

And if Sage believed she would remain beyond his reach forever...

She was wrong.

A wicked smile tugged at his lips, cold and full of sinister promise.

The chains of immortality were already tightening around her.

And soon...

Sage would feel them bite.

Pilatus advanced with predatory grace, his footsteps silent on the cathedral's ancient stone floor. Each step echoed in Sage's mind, a phantom sound that pressed against her resolve. She remained steadfast, though the weight of the moment coiled around her like a tightening noose. Her spine was a rod of steel against the ornate chair he had offered — a throne carved from bone-white marble, smaller than his own, but no less oppressive.

A mockery of power.

The chair wasn't a gift. It was a gilded cage.

The air between them grew heavy, thick with unspoken desires and the suffocating weight of unrelenting control. Shadows stretched from the towering pillars, slithering toward her feet as if they, too, sought to ensnare her.

"Consider it my gift to you," Pilatus murmured, his voice a velvet rumble that resonated through the oppressive silence. His words were a caress laced with poison. "A chair, fit for an empress. An empress who can guide the people to a better future. One who can witness the unfolding of history... for eternity."

His eyes, hungry and red like pools of endless blood, drank her in as though he could already see her seated beside him, immortal and bound to his empire. But Sage met his gaze without flinching, her defiance a spark in the shadowed chamber.

"A gift?" Her lips curled into a smile, but it was a cold, dead thing, devoid of warmth. "Chains by another name." Her voice, though muted, echoed like a bell tolling in the vast chamber. "An empress is not free, Pilatus. She's shackled to an empire. Shackled to an emperor. Bound by duty, by expectation ... by your will."

Her words lashed out, but Pilatus did not recoil. Instead, his eyes gleamed with something darker, more primal. His admiration for her defiance was a sickness — a festering hunger that grew with every rejection.

He leaned in, closing the distance between them, the chill of his presence brushing against her skin like ice. Mere inches separated them, yet it felt as though an abyss stretched between their souls. The scent of him — ancient, intoxicating, and laced with the coppery tang of blood — filled her senses, an oppressive, stomach-turning reminder of what he was.

"You could be eternal, powerful," he murmured, his tone seductive, almost reverent. His voice echoed off the cathedral walls, the sound wrapping around her like the devil's incantation. "Imagine it, my Sage. Time bending to your will. Empires rising and falling beneath your gaze. No sickness. No death. Only power ... everlasting."

The temptation slithered through his words like a serpent in the Garden, but Sage's resolve was a fortress built on the ashes of her suffering.

Her jaw tightened, her green eyes hard as emeralds. "I choose mortality," she hissed, her rejection crystalline and sharp enough to cut through the air between them. "Life is precious because it ends, Pilatus. I won't trade my soul for your cursed immortality."

Her words were a death knell, echoing off the stone walls, and for a fleeting moment, Sage saw something — a flicker in Pilatus's gaze. *Respect.*

It vanished as swiftly as it materialized; the void consuming all vestiges of his humanity. He masked it with practiced indifference, but Sage had seen the crack in his façade. A tiny fissure ... but a weakness, nonetheless.

"Very well," he murmured, though the chill in his voice belied the calm of his words. "We will try again ... another day."

The promise in his tone was not an idle one. It was a vow, a sinister oath that reverberated through the air like a distant drum of war. His eyes lingered on her for a moment too long, as if he were memorizing the contours of her defiance, savoring it before it crumbled.

"Your mood," he added, his lips curling into a dangerous smirk, "would improve if you ate something, my Sage."

The possessive emphasis on *my* sent a chill down her spine, but Sage refused to let him see her falter. Her silence was her weapon, a shield that Pilatus could not penetrate — yet.

As he straightened, withdrawing like a predator biding its time, the tension in the room did not dissipate. It thickened, swirling around Sage like a shroud of invisible chains. She felt them tightening, linking her to him, to this empire built on blood and deceit.

But chains could be broken.

And Pilatus would learn that her spirit was forged from something far stronger than steel.

Pilatus watched as Victor led her away, his expression unreadable — but inside, a storm raged.

The game was far from over and he reminded himself that he had all the time in the world to play it.

Victor's grip was unyielding, his hand a cold vise on Sage's shoulder as he guided her through the shadowed corridors of the cathedral. The ancient stones pressed in around her, their silence heavier than words, as if the walls themselves whispered secrets of power and betrayal. Each step echoed off the vaulted ceiling, a ghostly reminder of her entrapment.

The weight of her exchange with Pilatus still hung heavy on her mind. Every word, every glance, had been a move in their deadly game — a game where the stakes were far higher than she was prepared to admit. She had seen the glint of obsession in his eyes, felt the heat of his desire cloaked beneath promises of power and eternity.

But obsession was a double-edged sword.

If she played it right, she could twist his fixation into a weapon, a dagger aimed straight at the heart of his empire. Pilatus' obsession with her revealed a weakness, a flaw in his otherwise impenetrable armor. Yet as Victor led her deeper into the bowels of the cathedral, doubt slithered through her thoughts, coiling around her resolve like a serpent.

What if I'm wrong?

The door to her cell groaned as it swung open, the sound scraping against her nerves. As it clanged shut behind her, the finality echoed in her chest, sealing her within the suffocating confines of stone and shadow.

Sage pressed her palm to the cool wall, feeling the faint vibrations pulsing through the stone. The cathedral *breathed* — an ancient, living thing that bore witness to the unholy acts committed within its heart. It felt ... aware. Watching. Waiting.

Her mind spun, tracing the web of Pilatus's manipulations. His desires were not straightforward. His obsession with her was tangled, layered with contradictions that made it impossible to discern where control ended and genuine fascination began. He offered her a throne, but she recognized it as a gilded cage.

But why?

A shiver ran down her spine as a chilling realization seeped into her bones. Pilatus wasn't offering her power out of love, nor even lust. His interest in her was darker, more twisted — a game of domination where even Sage couldn't tell if she was the predator ... or the prey.

What if he knows?

The unsettling thought gnawed at her mind. What if Pilatus had already seen through her façade, already expected her attempt to manipulate him?

What if his obsession wasn't a weakness, but a trap designed to ensnare her?

Sage's heart pounded in her chest, her breath hitching as the walls seemed to close in.

I have to be sure.

Because if Pilatus was three steps ahead, she wasn't the hunter.

She was the prize.

And in this game, losing meant more than death — it meant eternity in his grasp.

THE GOSPEL OF BLOOD AND LIES

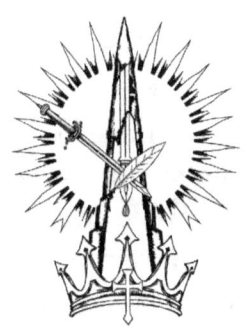

Sage's breath tore from her lungs in ragged gasps, slicing through the oppressive silence of the cell. Her eyes flew open, wide and wild, as if her nightmares had clawed their way into waking life. The echoes of her dream still lingered, a sickening imprint of Pilatus's eyes — those cold, luminous pools of blue that devoured her sanity inch by inch. In her mind, she felt his fangs sinking into her throat, not just draining her blood but siphoning her very essence, feeding on her fears, her will, her soul.

Her pulse hammered against her temples. The air in the cell was thick, stagnant, suffocating. Shadows crawled across the stone walls, stretching long fingers toward her, whispering echoes of her darkest thoughts. The cracked stone was as cold as a grave, and the damp chill seeped through the thin fabric of her socks, gnawing at her bones.

Get up.

Her body begged to stay where it was — curled, protected, hiding from the nightmare that had long since bled into her waking hours. But Sage Steel had never been one to cower, and she wouldn't start now. Her fingers dug into her palms, nails biting deep, grounding her as pain replaced the numbness. She welcomed it. Pain meant she was still alive. Pain meant Pilatus hadn't won.

Not yet.

Her breath steadied, though her heart still pounded with the force of a war drum. Rising to her feet, she moved toward the battered desk that stood like a lone sentinel in the cramped space. The desk was more than furniture — it was her altar, her weapon, her battlefield. The laptop's glow was an eerie beacon in the darkness, illuminating the scraps of paper scattered like fallen soldiers across the surface. Stubs of pencils, worn down from relentless scribbling, lay like spent bullets.

This was where she fought.

And tonight ... tonight she would strike.

Sage's fingers brushed the keyboard, her touch reverent, as if invoking a divine force. The words she was about to type would change everything — not just for her, but for humanity itself. She closed her eyes for a moment, drawing in a breath that carried the scent of damp stone and desperation. Her thoughts sharpened, her resolve hardening into steel.

Let them try to silence this.

Her fingers flew across the keys, the tap-tap-tap echoing like distant gunfire. Her manifesto unfolded, each word a dagger plunged into the heart of Pilatus's empire.

THE GOSPEL OF BLOOD AND LIES

By The Wraith

Once, in a time before the Crimson Reign, three men of influence and power conspired against the divine. Pilatus, Ananos, and Herod Antipas. Their names would echo through history, wrapped in deceit, wicked acts, and ultimately, veiled by time. In their time, they were men of stature, trusted by their people, yet their hearts were blackened by an insatiable thirst for dominion. Their hunger was not for mortal riches, but for something far greater — and far more sinister.

And in pursuit of quenching this evil craving, they committed a monstrous sacrilege.

They did not merely crucify the Son of God. They consumed Him.

In the dead of night, under a sky thick with the weight of betrayal, they gathered around a table not of communion, but of corruption. Silver and gold adorned the space, mocking the purity of what lay before them — Jesus Christ Himself, his dead body bound and broken. His blood seeped into the wood of the table, a silent witness to the greatest atrocity ever conceived.

Pilatus was the first to act. His dagger, forged not from steel but from treachery, pierced holy flesh with a precision born of malice.

Ananos and Herod followed, their hands eager to partake in the sacrilege that would grant them immortality.

It was not bread they broke that night — it was the flesh of the divine.

With each unholy bite, they damned themselves, their souls twisted and warped by the sin they had embraced. Their bodies rejected death, but their humanity was consumed in the process.

What emerged was not gods ... but monsters.

Vampires.

Pilatus, the architect of this blasphemous pact, rose first — his eyes no longer reflecting the mercy of a ruler, but the predatory hunger of a beast. His skin, once kissed by the sun, grew cold and unyielding. Stolen divinity surged through his veins, tainted by his own wickedness.

Herod and Ananos followed, bound by their shared transgression. Together, they became the progenitors of a new race — they are not divine, not immortal, but abominations masquerading as immortals.

And thus began the Crimson Reign, an empire built on evil actions, sustained by blood, and maintained through generations of deception.

The Lie That Shaped the World

Pilatus would have you believe vampires are a superior species — beings chosen to inherit the earth.

To rule over and guide humans.

Chosen to live forever!

But the truth is far more grotesque.

They are not gods.

They are not immortal.

They are not even evolution.

They are thieves.

They stole their power from the Son of God, and they have spent centuries weaving lies to conceal their origins. Pilatus manipulates scripture, twisting the sacred to justify the profane. He has reshaped faith itself into a weapon, subjugating both humans and vampires alike under the yoke of his false divinity.

But lies can only hold for so long.

The Time for Reckoning is Now

Pilatus, Herod, and Ananos have ruled unchecked for too long. Their empire thrives on silence, on fear, on the belief that resistance is futile. They have carved the lands of the earth between them and enslaved us all!

In truth, they are murderers, cannibals, and blasphemers!

I, *The Wraith*, tell you this — the truth has power.

And truth ... will burn their empire to ash.

They fear the truth because it is the only weapon that can destroy them.

The truth is more excruciating than any stake. Sharper than any blade.

It cuts through the illusion they have built and lays bare the rot beneath.

And now, that truth is in your hands.

You have two choices: bare your throat to the butcher's knife, or take your freedom back!

Rise.

Resist.

Reclaim what was stolen.

God will bring His children together to cast down these false gods. He will breathe fire into the hearts of those who believe, and that fire will consume the empire of darkness.

Sage's fingers paused, hovering over the keys, her chest heaving with the weight of what she had just composed. The words burned on the screen, a beacon in the abyss of Pilatus's reign.

Her pulse pounded in her ears, the intensity of the moment pressing down on her. She had not merely written a manifesto. She had declared war.

But had she?

The truth was, a shadow war had been ongoing for more than a decade. With much of humanity just accepting what the vampires had told them, and only a few fighting back against them.

No, she was bringing a reckoning. A reckoning of light and truth.

The air in the cell was charged now, thick with an energy that hummed in her bones. For a moment, she allowed herself to lean back, to take in the magnitude of what she was doing.

Many humans were convinced that the elite vampires could not be killed. She knew different! They could all be killed!

With the truth in the open, the fight would no longer be confined to the shadows.

It would begin.

A distant echo of praetorian footsteps reached her ears, growing louder, heavier.

Sage's heart pounded, but her resolve did not waver. Her words would be set loose into the world, and soon, they would strike like lightning — igniting a blaze that would consume everything Pilatus had built.

Sage's fingers hovered above the keyboard, trembling with a cocktail of exhaustion and adrenaline. The glow of the screen cast an eerie pallor over her face, highlighting the sharp lines of tension etched into her features. Her breaths came in shallow, controlled measures, but her heart pounded like a war drum in her chest. This moment — this keystroke — would change everything.

The laptop hummed softly, a mechanical heartbeat in the otherwise suffocating silence of her cell. The faint glow of the screen was the only light in the dim space, flickering like a dying star, as if the machine itself sensed the magnitude of the task it was about to undertake.

Her pulse echoed in her ears as she typed, each keystroke a whisper that echoed through the tomb-like stillness of her prison.

> Accessing darknet channels...

> Establishing secure uplink...

> Encrypting message...

The dark web — a shadow realm that pulsed beneath the surface of the internet — came alive before her eyes. Lines of code unfolded across the screen like veins spreading through the body of a sleeping beast. She navigated the intricate pathways with ease, her fingers dancing across the keys as if guided by instinct. Each line of code was a step deeper into forbidden territory, a descent into the abyss, where secrecy and rebellion thrived.

Sage's eyes narrowed, her focus unrelenting as she worked her way toward the contact who had been her unseen lifeline: Fang-hater.

Her ally. Her accomplice.

The phantom who lurked in the digital shadows, feeding her bits of crucial information, helping her spread seeds of insurrection. She had never met him — or her — but trust in this faceless ally had been forged through coded messages and a shared hatred for Pilatus's regime. Whoever they were, they had the means to amplify her voice, to carry her manifesto across continents and through encrypted channels where no vampire surveillance could follow.

> Connected to Fang-hater

> Protocol Ready

Her fingers hesitated for the briefest of moments, hovering above the keys. Doubt, insidious and cold, whispered from the corners of her mind.

What if they track it?

What if Fang-hater has been compromised?

What if this is the moment Pilatus has been waiting for?

But Sage shoved those thoughts aside. There was no turning back now. The truth needed to be unleashed. Even if the cost was her life.

Her jaw clenched as her fingers typed the ultimate words: "Start dissemination protocol."

The phrase was clinical, but its meaning was far more profound.

It was a declaration of war.

With one final keystroke, Sage unleashed her narrative into the ether. Her words, infused with the weight of centuries of deceit, slipped through the cracks of the digital realm like a serpent in the grass — unseen, unheard, but deadly.

> Uploading...

> Data Packet Dispersed

> Status: Active

The message fragmented and multiplied, scattering across countless servers and relays, its encrypted tendrils spreading like a virus through the veins of the internet. Even Pilatus's vast network of surveillance couldn't stop it now.

Sage exhaled, her breath shaky, her body thrumming with a mixture of relief and dread.

It's out.

Her manifesto was no longer just words on a screen — it was a spark that would ignite a wildfire. It would spread like an uncontrollable blaze through the digital underworld, reaching eyes that had long been blind and ears that had forgotten how to listen.

Fang-hater would see to that.

Closer than she realized, in a damp stone room beneath the ruins of a once-bustling city, a lone figure hunched over a cluster of monitors, the glow of the screens illuminating a face half-hidden by the shadows of a tattered hood. The air was thick with the scent of stale coffee, cigarettes and burned circuits, a claustrophobic blend that mirrored the tension crackling in the atmosphere.

A notification blinked on the center screen — "Message Received."

The figure's lips curled into a satisfied grin as gloved fingers flew over the keyboard, eyes scanning the encrypted message. Lines of code unraveled like an ancient scroll, revealing the manifesto Sage had crafted with her blood, sweat, and unyielding defiance.

"She did it ... she finally realized the truth."

Fang-hater's gaze darkened as the manifesto loaded, line by line, *The Gospel of Blood and Lies.*

For a moment, the room seemed to hold its breath. The words burned across the screen, each sentence a blade poised to slice through the heart of the Crimson Empire. As the weight of Sage's revelation settled in Fang-hater's mind, something ... shifted.

A chill ran down their spine, one not born of fear but of realization.

Pilatus would feel this.

He wouldn't just read these words — he would feel them. Deep in the marrow of his immortal bones, where his cursed soul was chained to the crime that birthed his existence, he would sense this disturbance.

His instincts, honed over millennia, would recoil at the power of truth unleashed.

For Pilatus, this wasn't merely a threat.

It was prophecy.

The ancient predator within him would recognize that his empire had been pierced by a weapon he could not control — not steel, not fire, but something far more dangerous.

Faith.

Fang-hater's lips pressed into a grim line, their pulse quickening with anticipation. They had witnessed revolutions sparked by anger, by desperation.

But this? This was something different.

This was a war fueled by belief, by the righteous fury of the oppressed.

Pilatus had built his empire on the bones of the divine — and now that foundation was fracturing.

"Damn, Sage..." the deep voice murmured softly, almost reverently. "You just declared a holy war."

Without hesitation, Fang-hater started the dissemination protocol, setting the wheels in motion. Automated scripts spread the message to encrypted forums, private networks, and shadowed corners of the internet where rebels, dissidents, and those who had suffered under the Crimson Empire would find it.

> Protocol Engaged

> Dissemination Across 300+ Nodes

> Estimated Worldwide Spread: 72 Hours

The message was no longer confined to Sage's cell, and Fang-hater's server — it was free now, an unstoppable force surging through cyberspace, carried by the digital winds to every corner where rebellion simmered just beneath the surface.

As the protocols executed flawlessly, Fang-hater leaned back, the faint glow of the monitors reflecting off the edge of a wicked grin.

"Let's light this match," they whispered, their voice laced with grim determination.

And somewhere, they knew that in the farthest recesses of Pilatus's cold, undead heart ... the first ember of dread began to smolder.

Sage stared blankly at the blinking cursor on the screen, her pulse gradually slowing but her mind racing. The air in her cell was heavier now, charged with the weight of what she had done.

Her body sagged, exhaustion clawing at her bones, but she refused to let herself succumb to it.

Not yet.

The faint echo of footsteps reverberated down the corridor — measured, unhurried, but with a weight that spoke of authority.

Victor.

Sage's jaw clenched. She knew that sound, knew the man who walked those halls like a reaper in waiting.

Pilatus's enforcer. His shadow.

"Time's up..." she whispered to herself, her voice barely audible in the oppressive stillness.

She closed her eyes for a moment, steeling herself.

The first blow had been struck.

Now ... let the empire burn.

As the footsteps grew louder, Sage's lips curled into the faintest, defiant smile.

Let him come.

As the footsteps stopped outside her cell, Sage whispered to the darkness, "Let them come. Let them choke on the truth."

The real war had already begun.

And this time...

Truth would not die.

THE SPARK THAT BURNS EMPIRES

IN THE DAPPLED SHADOWS of human enclaves, where hope had long since withered, the flicker of rebellion reignited. Screens, old and cracked, flickered to life, casting an eerie glow on faces etched with hardship and fear. The blue light danced across hollowed cheeks and tired eyes, reflecting not just desperation but something far more dangerous — fury.

"Can you believe this?" A woman's voice, roughened by years of whispered resistance, trembled with fury as she read aloud from a battered tablet. Her audience, a cluster of resistance fighters huddled in a derelict subway station, leaned closer, the stale air thick with anticipation. The damp concrete walls, cracked and crumbling, seemed to close in, as though the city itself was listening.

"Pilatus... that monster," she spat, her voice a jagged whisper. "He's been playing God after killing God."

The words echoed in the chamber, vibrating through the rusted steel of forgotten train tracks as they read: The Gospel of Blood and Lies. Each syllable sliced through the decade of oppression like a blade, peeling back the rot that had festered under Pilatus's reign.

"Christ's body?" Another murmured, his voice choked with disgust. His hands clenched so tightly around a rusted crowbar that his knuckles turned bone white. "This ... this is blasphemy. Sacrilege!"

A shiver ran through the gathered crowd as the revelation sank in. Eyes, once dulled by despair, now gleamed with something that had long been extinguished — purpose.

"They didn't just kill Him ..." the woman's voice cracked, her lips quivering as tears welled in her eyes. "They devoured Him."

Gasps echoed through the space, the charged air thickening as the weight of the truth settled over them. Pilatus and his unholy brethren had built their empire atop the bones of God Himself. The enormity of the revelation pressed down on them, but beneath the horror, something stirred. Something primal.

"If they killed him ... they can be killed too." Others murmured.

"Spread the word," the woman commanded, her voice a vow that echoed with the conviction of a martyr. "Let it be known. Our overlords are not gods! Let them feel our wrath."

The others nodded, their eyes reflecting not just anger but righteous zealotry. The ember of rebellion had been rekindled, and now it burned with the fury of divine vengeance.

"This ends now."

The words echoed off the damp walls, swallowed by the darkness beyond — but the message had already taken root. And in the hearts of the oppressed, that seed of truth grew, spreading tendrils of defiance that would soon strangle the empire that had fed on their souls for too long.

The grandeur of the Washington National Cathedral had once stood as a monument to faith, but now its hollowed halls echoed with whispers of doubt. The sacred space, once revered, had become a mausoleum where shadows stretched long and sinister, devouring what little sanctity remained.

The vampire elites, once happily unified under the iron rule of Pilatus, now murmured with unease, their voices slithering through the darkness like serpents.

"Have you read it?" one hissed, his voice barely audible above the somber chants echoing through the vaulted stone archways.

"Every word," another murmured, his tone laced with a venomous edge. The age-old blood within him simmered with unrest. "It questions everything we are. Destroys the image of our invulnerability."

"Do you think it's true?" Another whispered even lower.

The flickering candlelight cast distorted shadows on their pale faces, reflecting the turmoil within. Doubt, once an unforgivable weakness, now spread like a plague among them.

"Could the humans rally against us?" A fourth vampire pondered, his voice hushed but laced with a nervous tremor. His eyes, like molten silver, darted toward the stained-glass windows as though expecting a horde of zealots to come crashing through.

And there, sitting amidst the discordant symphony of his court, was Pilatus.

His expression was a mask of composed indifference, but the cold light in his eyes betrayed the tempest raging beneath. Pilatus's fingers curled over the armrests of his throne, the ivory grooves carved into the ancient stone worn smooth by centuries of clenched fists.

This narrative — his story told in a light he could not control — was a toxin in his bloodstream, threatening the collapse of his dominion.

He knew who was to blame, even if the others did not.

What he did not know was how Sage had passed the information to this 'Wraith'.

But he would find out.

"Contain it," he commanded, his voice a chilling calm that cut through the murmurings like a scalpel. His Night Sentinels, clad in obsidian armor, stood motionless, awaiting his orders. "Silence the dissenters. I will not have my empire crumble over the ramblings of an online heretic."

The General of the Night Sentinels stepped forward, his face emotionless, but his eyes gleamed with predatory intent. He struck his chest with a clenched fist in the old way and disappeared into the shadows.

But even as Pilatus's lieutenants moved with swift obedience, the seeds of doubt had already taken root.

Beneath their practiced veneer of loyalty, cracks began to form in the foundation of Pilatus's dominion. *The Wraith's* words had become the chink in their armor, a whisper that echoed in the minds of even the most faithful. The whisper of vulnerability and stolen powers in the night promised a coming dawn of upheaval.

And Pilatus felt it.

Like the tightening of a noose.

As the disbelief and suspicion grew throughout the empire, Sage remained in her cell, unaware of the shockwaves her words had sent rippling through both districts and cathedrals alike. But even in isolation, she felt the shift in the air. The sounds of rapidly marching, booted feet were a prelude to the chaos that was to come. And with anxious breath, she waited for the world to turn.

Pilatus's silhouette loomed over the flickering screen, his countenance a mask of barely restrained fury as Ananos and Herod Antipas appeared via video conference. The two advisors, immortal conspirators who had stood by his side since the night of the betrayal, sat cloaked in shadow, their expressions carved from stone but tight with apprehension.

"Every resource at our disposal must be employed to quash this insurrection before it begins," Pilatus commanded, his fingers steepled tightly, his posture betraying none of the storm brewing within. "I want online and other surveillance doubled. No ... tripled. We must contain the spread of this ... this libel."

The screen crackled slightly. The connection strained as though the weight of their words disturbed the air itself.

Ananos, his eyes glinting with a cold calculation that spoke of centuries of merciless cunning, inclined his head. "The human networks will be monitored. We will deal harshly with any sympathizers within our ranks."

Herod Antipas, ever the strategist, leaned forward, his face partially obscured by the flicker of his own screen. "And the source of these writings?" His voice was laced with a dread that mirrored the unrest among their kind. "There are few who know the details of the beginning."

A moment of silence followed, thick and oppressive.

"A human spread this ... with a vampire source," Herod murmured, his tone grave. "There are radicals on both sides. If they join forces..." His words trailed off, leaving the unspoken threat hanging in the air like a guillotine. "We must cut off the head of this serpent before it poisons us all."

"Indeed," Pilatus's jaw clenched, a muscle ticking in his cheek as his icy gaze pierced through the distance separating them. He was reminded of the pressure he had felt from them both on the sentencing of Christ.

He would not give up his Sage in the same way.

He had not broken her yet.

"Begin with the human territories," Pilatus said, his voice low but carrying the weight of impending doom. "Leave no stone unturned."

And with a decisive click, the screen went black.

But the darkness that followed was not empty.

It was heavy with the promise of blood.

Back in her cell, Sage's hands hovered above the keyboard, the faint glow casting an ethereal light across her pale features. Her body was taut, her muscles coiled with a tension that echoed the storm building outside these walls.

A soft ping announced the arrival of a new message — coded, encrypted, and known only to her and Fang-hater.

Her pulse quickened as her eyes scanned the line of text that flickered onto the screen, each word amplifying the drumbeat of rebellion already resonating through the halls of power.

"Your words have wings," the message read, "and the world is listening."

A shiver ran down her spine. It wasn't fear that gripped her ... not exactly. It was the weight of knowing that she had unleashed a force that could not be contained.

Until it was over. One way or another.

Sage's lips curled into a small, weary smile, but it was a smile laced with trepidation. She had known the risks, understood the consequences, yet the gravity of what she had set in motion pressed down upon her now like a heavy chain.

There was no way that Pilatus did not know by now who was the catalyst of the truth being spread far and wide.

"God, help me," she whispered under her breath, her fingers clenched together as she prayed.

Beyond the cold stone walls of her prison, rebellion stirred. Pilatus's empire trembled. And the whisper of revolution became a roar that echoed in places even he couldn't reach.

A reckoning was coming.

And as the distant sound of booted footsteps echoed down the corridor, Sage braced herself.

The storm was no longer on the horizon.

It had already begun.

THE GREAT ESCAPE

Danny's hand, slick with blood and trembling with adrenaline, instinctively grasped the hilt of his machete as he and his fellow insurgent crept out from the shadows to rejoin his brother and the three other members of their team. Deep black stains splattered their clothing like macabre brushstrokes, glinting eerily under the pale light filtering down from the cathedral's towering spires.

Tommy's gaze met Danny's — a silent exchange loaded with tension and unspoken words. His eyes, cold and calculating, scanned them for any sign of failure.

"Any problems?" His voice was a whisper, barely disturbing the suffocating stillness around them.

"We cut them off without detection," Danny murmured, but his tone lacked conviction. His eyes lingered too long on the blood staining his machete, avoiding Tommy's unrelenting stare.

Tommy's jaw clenched, his expression a mask of grim resolve. He gave a curt nod, silently commanding the group to move out.

They slithered through the city's decaying underbelly, navigating dark, forgotten alleys and collapsed buildings toward their target — the Washington National Cathedral. Its jagged spires clawed at the heavens like skeletal fingers, looming over the city with malevolent grace. The pre-dawn darkness painted the ancient structure in shades of menace, a mausoleum of secrets and death.

Every step felt heavier than the last. The oppressive silence weighed down on them like a shroud. The air, thick with the scent of decay and mildew, clung to their skin as they moved through the forgotten veins of the city. Though they had relied on Eli's and the hacktivists' information, a gnawing sense of unease coiled around Danny's gut.

The information they had received was a razor-sharp, double-edged weapon, capable of both aiding and destroying them with one wrong move. A single misstep could unravel their entire operation, putting them at the mercy of the vampires.

What if they had been misled?

What if this was another trap?

As they passed the outer defenses, unseen yet feeling exposed, the tension wound tight around them. Resolve was etched into the grim lines of their faces, a shared understanding that the necessity of their mission outweighed the cost of their deeds.

A distant clang echoed, a ghostly sound that might have been footsteps or the rattling of chains, setting their nerves jangling. Light flickered somewhere ahead — a patrol, perhaps, or an automated searchlight scanning for intruders.

Tommy's hand rose, signaling a stop. Shadows danced across the stone walls as a beam of light swept past — a lone sentry patrolling the perimeter. They pressed themselves against the cold stone, their breath held as the light drifted away.

"Move," Tommy whispered, his voice barely audible.

The cathedral's walls loomed closer, swallowing them into its embrace. The cold, ancient stones exhaled an icy chill that seeped into their bones.

As they crept inside, the cathedral's innards transformed into a different, sinister beast. The cold stone walls towered above them, oozing with the weight of centuries and the icy grip of abandonment. Whispers echoed up and down the stone corridors, carrying ancient secrets and promising imminent danger. It was as if the catacombs were alive and intent on suffocating them within their ancient burial chambers.

The harsh, metallic screech of the lock being forced open ripped through the oppressive silence, a jarring intrusion that sent adrenaline pumping through their veins. The meager light from the corridor spilled into Sage's cell, revealing its bleak austerity and its solitary prisoner, who seemed so out of place amidst the pandemonium beyond.

Sage lifted her gaze from her work, her eyes catching the torchlight and reflecting it back like twin emerald lighthouses in a stormy sea. They flickered between Danny and Tommy, scanning their faces in shock for signs of imminent danger. The papers on her desk fluttered to the stone floor, forgotten in the sudden draft created by the door's violent opening. A moment hung suspended in time, as if reality itself was holding its breath.

Her heart pounded, uncertainty knotting her stomach as her vision adjusted to the figures standing before her. For a breathless moment, she thought her mind had conjured them as part of another cruel hallucination.

"Mom," Danny choked out, his voice thick with a torrent of emotions that transcended mere recognition.

Sage's breath hitched as she crossed the small space, her movements swift despite the fatigue that had hollowed her out. She pulled her sons into her arms, holding them as if afraid they would vanish if she loosened her grip.

Relief, terror, resolve — all these emotions swirled together in this chaotic reunion.

"My God! How did you get past Victor?" Her voice wavered with worry as she stepped back to scrutinize them, then looked to the others waiting beyond the open cell door.

"Victor?" Tommy's expression darkened. "There was no guard outside."

Sage stiffened. Her mind raced. No guard? That wasn't right. Her pulse quickened, a fresh wave of anxiety slamming into her.

"That means we have even less time than I thought." Her voice was urgent now, her body already moving toward the door. "We need to leave. Now!"

Their reunion was cut short, the warmth of it drowned beneath the weight of danger pressing in from all sides. They moved swiftly, retracing their path through the shadowed corridors, but the claustrophobic maze of the cathedral seemed more treacherous now. Every turn felt like a trap waiting to spring.

"Hurry," Tommy growled under his breath, urging them faster while his hand guided Sage protectively.

Danny kept watch over his shoulder, alert for any threats. Their mother was the linchpin of their plan, the reason for this audacious raid into the heart of the vampire empire, and they would defend her with their lives.

The distant wail of alarms punctured the air, bouncing around the stone walls like the metallic ball of an old-fashioned pinball machine, growing deafening with each passing heartbeat. The sound of their

subterfuge crumbling, of the enemy being roused, fueled their desperation and quickened their pace.

"We're almost there," Danny whispered hoarsely, glancing at Sage,
who responded with a nod; determination etched deep into her
features. Tommy felt the enormity of what they were doing press
down on him - the lives gambled and blood already spilled in this
daring endeavor. They had come too far to falter now; the bitter taste
of ashes in his mouth was a grim testament to the sacrifices made by
all of them. Then, just as freedom seemed within reach, a sudden
explosion of dim light poured through windows of stained glass set
high in the Cathedral ceilings, announcing the coming of dawn.

Just another 1000 yards and they would be in the sunlight's safety.

"Go!" Sage gasped out between coughs as the tunnel seemed to
shudder and dust rained down on their frantic escape.

A horrendous screeching noise filled the air as they realized the
vampires were attempting to close the entrance gates that hadn't
been used in a decade.

They raced toward the underground garage entrance; light at tunnel's end offering a stark contrast to the darkness behind them. Yet
even as freedom beckoned tantalizingly close, the pursuing shadows
that clung stubbornly to them were a chilling reminder of the danger
still hot on their heels.

Sage's worn shoe snagged on a rogue cobblestone, pitching her forward into Tommy's back while Danny lunged from the rear, his firm grip arresting her fall.

It was minor, just a slight misstep, but the moment her foot twisted, pain surged through her body like wildfire. Instinctively, she caught herself, her hand flying to her mouth to stifle a cry.

But the moment her fingers brushed her lips, a chilling realization gripped her.

No...

Her fingertips brushed against something foreign — elongated. Sharp.

Fangs.

"Mom?" Danny's voice, strained with concern, cut through the turmoil. His gaze locked on hers, and in that instant, he saw what she tried to hide.

A deathly silence engulfed them.

Tommy froze, his eyes narrowing as they took in the horrifying truth. "What ... what the fuck?"

A deathly hush descended upon Sage as she locked eyes with her sons, their faces etched with dawning horror. "Pilatus," she began, her voice barely audible against the oppressive silence of the cathedral crypts, "that fucker has damned me. God, I swear, I didn't know."

Tommy jerked back as if struck by a bolt of lightning; his features twisted in a grotesque mask of shock and denial. "What are you saying?"

Sage's throat worked, but no words came. Finally, she forced the cursed word from her lips — a word that shattered the last remnants of hope.

"Vampire."

The word echoed in the space between them, a dagger slicing through their hearts.

Tommy's face twisted, a mask of denial and anguish. "No ... no, that's not possible."

"I didn't know..." Sage whispered, her voice barely audible as her fingers brushed the fangs again, her expression crumbling. "I swear ... I didn't know."

The boys had heard tales whispered in hushed tones and seen the grisly aftermath left in the wake of family members of the rebels who were unlucky enough to be turned instead of killed, but never did they imagine that this monstrous fate would befall their own mother.

Danny's jaw clenched, his mind warring between duty and love. His machete hung loosely in his grip, but his knuckles were white from the tension.

They had fought so long to destroy monsters like her ... how could they now protect her?

"Concentrate," she commanded, her voice hardened by years of battle. "We've got to get out of here or we are all fucked." Her voice might have been soft, but it carried an iron resolve that had guided them through countless insurrections.

Tommy's mind spun with the horror of the truth. Their own flesh and blood turned into one of the very monsters they had pledged to destroy. But despite the gut-wrenching realization, he could not falter in their mission, not now.

They could not leave her here; she knew too much about everything.

A beat passed.

"Move!" Tommy barked, his voice raw with a tumult of emotion.

Sage shoved down her fear, falling into step between her sons, her mind a whirlwind of horror and resolve. She was no longer just a prisoner. She was a liability ... a threat.

And if she lost control ... they would be the ones to pay the price.

The antechamber near the garage exit was a war zone of chaos. The metallic scent of blood and scorched flesh saturated the air as the rebels fought the small patrol against the closing gate — a last-ditch attempt by the vampires to trap them before they could escape.

The vampires descended like shadows torn from nightmares — claws glinting, eyes blazing, mouths wet with hunger. One leaped from a second-story ledge above the antechamber, landing with a wet crunch atop a rebel, driving its claws through the man's shoulder. Blood sprayed across the concrete like crimson mist.

Tommy turned with a roar, his silver-edged blade whistling through the air. The vampire raised its arm to block, but the sword cleaved through flesh and bone with a screech, sending the severed limb flying as the creature shrieked in pain.

"Hold the line!" Another rebel bellowed, teeth bared in defiance, his twin daggers gleaming. He ducked beneath a lunging male vamp, jammed one blade into its abdomen, and dragged it upward until ribs cracked open like rotten wood. The second dagger pierced the base of its skull, silencing it mid-scream.

Danny rolled beneath a snarling vampire's outstretched arms, kicked out one of its knees with a sickening pop, then vaulted up and slammed an iron stake into its back, driving it through the heart. The creature convulsed, black veins spider-webbing across its skin before it collapsed in a heap of tangled limbs and bloody gore.

A rebel with a small flamethrower ignited a cluster of vamps attempting to flank them from the shadows. Fire roared to life, illuminating their shrieking forms as they writhed in agony, the scent of burning leather and seared flesh overwhelming the air. Another rebel was seized mid-run, dragged screaming into the dark, his shrieks abruptly silenced with a wet crunch.

"Push through!" Tommy shouted, slamming his foot into a vampire's chest hard enough to crack its sternum. "We're almost there!"

Sage whirled, her fangs exposed, eyes burning like green fire. A vampire lunged — she caught it by the throat and drove its head through a steel support beam, splattering gore across the wall. Her hands shook, her breath ragged — from rage, hunger, or guilt, even she couldn't say.

The battle raged around them, every heartbeat a countdown, every scream a testament to the price of survival. The rebels fought like demons — not for glory, but for escape; for survival. Ahead of them, the gate began to groan, metal shrieking against metal.

They had seconds. Maybe less.

A vampire, clad in the intimidating obsidian body armor of the Night Sentinels, grappled with the intricate mechanisms of the colossal subterranean garage door that hadn't moved since the vampires had conquered the world a decade ago. His movements were erratic and desperate as he yanked and clawed at a frozen control lever adorned with a crimson knob trying to cut off the rebels' escape. The metallic scrape of his actions echoed menacingly through the vast underground space as the rusted metal garage door chunked and chunked back and forth in place.

Danny lunged forward wondering if he would stop the fanger in time, but before he could strike, Sage's hand shot out, her grip vice-like as it halted him.

"No," she hissed, her voice guttural and cold.

She reached down swiftly to Danny's belt, her fingers closing around an iron stake — cold and lethal. In one fluid motion, she hurled the stake with deadly accuracy toward their adversary.

With unerring precision, it found its mark - embedding itself deep within the vampire's eye socket and burst through the back of his skull, in a wide burst of vitreous humor, blood, and brain matter.

The bulls-eye was a testament to Sage's continued swift and deadly accuracy with throwing weapons.

The sentinel crumpled to the cold concrete floor, collapsing under his own weight like a Punch puppet, whose strings had been abruptly severed.

They looked around to see the bodies of the vampires all dead.

"Jesus..." Danny whispered, his voice filled with a mixture of awe and dread.

Sage turned, covered in the gore of her kills, her fangs gleaming in the dim light, her lips curled in grim satisfaction.

"That felt ... good," she murmured, her voice laced with something darker — something dangerous.

The revelation sent shockwaves through the rebels accompanying the Steel family. Hands gravitated towards belts laden with iron stakes and silvered knives, but before panic could take root fully, followed by violence, Tommy's voice sliced through their startled silence.

"Stand down!" His command echoed with raw authority. His piercing gaze swept over them. "This is still *The Wraith*."

The rebels' hesitation lingered, but Tommy's word was law.

The antechamber near the garage exit offered a fleeting moment of relief, just enough time to steel themselves for the final mad dash to freedom. The shrieking alarms echoed like banshees in the distance, their urgency increasing as the bloodthirsty vampire guards closed in on their location. What was meant to be a covert mission now turned into a clamorous, desperate race against the clock and razor-sharp fangs.

"Stay close," Tommy commanded, his voice rough with unspoken fear as he checked the magazine of his pistol; one of the few left in the resistance; bullets being more precious than diamonds. The huge garage space buzzed with the tension of a storm about to break. Every shadow was a potential threat, every sound a possible attack.

They edged toward the exit, the first rays of sunlight teasing their vision. Yet even the promise of safety was overshadowed by the dread of what lay behind them.

"Ready?" Sage asked, her new reality momentarily pushed aside by the instinct to survive.

"Always," came the unified response from her sons.

Tommy and Danny exchanged a look, a silent vow passing between them. No matter what awaited outside those cathedral walls, they would face it together; as a family.

THE SACRIFICE AND REVELATION

THE BLARING OF ALARMS and distant shouts echoed through the stone corridors, chasing after the small group of rebels as they huddled in the shadowed alcove next to the bay doors. Sage, her heart pounding with a chaotic rhythm that matched the blood thundering through her veins, crouched low beside her sons. But this time, it wasn't just adrenaline that made her pulse race.

It was hunger.

A hunger that gnawed at her from the inside, curling through her veins like a serpent tightening its coils. The ache transcended a simple pain; it was a dark, insidious craving, promising power and satisfaction if she would only give in.

The scent of blood filled her senses. She could hear it — the steady thrum of heartbeats around her. Tommy. Danny. Their comrades. Each pulse resonated, a siren song luring her closer to the edge.

Control it. Sage clenched her jaw, her nails biting into her palms as she fought the overwhelming urge to feed.

"Move," hissed one of the rebels, his voice barely above a whisper, but the urgency was palpable. "We have to move now."

Sage's head snapped up, her emerald eyes flashing unnervingly in the dim light. She gave a curt nod; her face a mask of composure, though the storm inside her raged unchecked. She could feel her body changing, her instincts screaming to embrace what she had become.

They crept toward the exit, each step a battle to maintain control. Sage's foot caught on a loose stone, sending her stumbling. Her hand shot out to brace against the ancient wall, but the moment her palm brushed against the sunlight spilling through a narrow crack, a searing pain lanced through her.

Sizzle.

Her flesh blistered, and the acrid scent of burning skin wafted through the air.

Sage recoiled, her breath catching in her throat as she cradled her wounded hand, crimson streaking her pale fingers.

"Are you okay?" Tommy's voice was barely above a whisper, concern lacing every word.

"I'm fine," Sage lied, her voice steady despite the agony that pulsed through her palm. But it wasn't the pain that rattled her — what rocked her was the realization that she couldn't go with them.

I can't.

Her thoughts churned as rapidly as her heart now did. Her sons, Tommy and Danny, fierce and brave leaders of the rebellion, would be endangered by her very existence. Now a blood-thirsty creature, she was an abomination to the cause she had birthed and nurtured

— a liability that could undermine everything they had fought for ... bled for ... died for.

The antechamber they traversed was a space caught between eras, the gothic arches above them framing the encroaching light of a new day — a day she could no longer greet without fear. Shadows clung to the corners like spirits of the past, whispering of the time before the world had plunged into this endless nightmare.

A resolve hardened in Sage's chest, heavier than the stone cathedral that surrounded her. She wouldn't let her affliction become the rebellion's downfall. Her gaze swept over her sons and soldiers, each carrying the weight of hope for humanity's future — a future that was no longer hers.

A singular, clear purpose took root in her mind, sinking its tentacles deep. Protect them ... protect the cause, even if it meant embracing the coldest hell possible. She could feel the pull of the coming daylight, an ominous reminder of the line she now walked between two worlds.

"Tommy, Danny," her voice was barely above a whisper, but it carried the weight of finality. As they approached the threshold where sunlight bled through the ancient stone, Sage turned to face her sons. Her eyes, shimmering with unshed tears, betrayed the war raging inside her. "I love you." Her voice cracked, the emotion straining against her resolve. "You need to know that you can win this war. But now ... you have to run. Run, live and fight another day."

"No," Danny growled, his jaw clenched, eyes wild with defiance. "No fucking way, Mom! We didn't come all this way just to leave you here."

"Baby," she told her youngest gently, touching his face softly. "I'm not staying here. I can't go with you. But I can buy you some time and some cover."

Tommy's face was a mask of stone, his green eyes distant, already trying to calculate the odds of survival. But Sage saw through the façade. He was breaking.

"Tommy..." she turned to him, her hand brushing softly against his cheek. "You have to let this out, baby. You can't keep it bottled up inside forever."

Tommy's lips parted, but no words came. The weight of the moment suffocated the air between them. She tenderly kissed him on the cheek.

"Now," Sage ordered softly, her voice tinged with a desperate urgency. "You need to go. All of you. That's an order."

They hesitated — just for a moment. But it was a moment too long.

"Run!" Sage's voice snapped like a whip, her tone commanding the obedience of soldiers hardened by war.

Their responses were choked, faces etched with confusion and pain, unable to comprehend the finality of their mother's tone. But there was no time for lingering goodbyes or explanations; the cost of delay was too high.

Reluctantly, they turned and dashed into the coming light, sprinting toward their vehicles parked in the ruins beyond.

"Go..." she murmured under her breath, her gaze locked on her sons as they disappeared into the rising dawn. "Triumph."

With a mother's fierce determination, Sage spun on her heel, turning her back to the fleeting safety her sons ran toward and dashed west to the cathedral's gaping entrance, keeping to the narrowing shadows.

The light of the morning sun spilled through the ruined archways of the cathedral, an unforgiving executioner awaiting her approach.

She stepped into the courtyard, the warmth of the sun brushing her skin like a lover's caress, as Night Sentinels in skin covering armor met her and surrounded her. While the Sentinels were protected, her once impervious skin was now vulnerable and exposed.

And then it began.

The pain was immediate and absolute.

The sun's merciless rays seared into Sage's vampiric flesh, each photon a blazing lance that pierced her transformed skin.

Blisters erupted across her skin, swelling and bursting with sickening pops that echoed in her ears. Her flesh split open, raw and bleeding, as the sun's unrelenting touch peeled away layer after layer. The scent of burning flesh filled her nostrils, thick and suffocating.

She screamed.

But not in fear. In defiance.

Her shrieks echoed off the cathedral's walls, a concert of agony that sent the Night Sentinels flinching away in horror. They had never witnessed such a sight. The sun, humanity's greatest weapon, was ravaging one of their own — and yet, Sage stood; not seeking the shadows, nor attempting to flee. She willingly stood ignited in a pyre of self-sacrifice.

The Night Sentinels, while still surrounding her, backed to a safe distance, forgetting the retreating rebels as they gazed in astonishment at how the sun's rays punished new vampire flesh.

Her dark auburn hair, once a vibrant cascade of waves, shriveled and crisped against the onslaught of sunlight. It curled up in tendrils of smoke that twisted away into the ever-brighter morning sky.

Her piercing green eyes boiled within their sockets, their luminescent beauty dimming under the sun's relentless assault. Yet they remained open, unwaveringly locked onto the distant figures of her sons as they ran for freedom and their lives, as if drawing strength from the very sight of them, giving her the power to give the last of herself.

The elegant lines of her statuesque figure convulsed in an erratic dance of agony as fire consumed her from within and without. Her once lean muscles contracted violently under the heat, pulling taut against bone until it seemed she might shatter from tension alone.

And yet through it all — through every excruciating second that stretched into eternity — Sage did not falter. She did not try to take cover or save herself. She stood firm amidst her flaming agony, bearing the unbearable with an iron will born from love and desperation. And she did not fall.

For this was her choice; this was her ultimate act for her children ... for humanity's salvation.

Her arms spread wide, palms up, a silent prayer to the heavens she had always believed in.

Forgive me. Let them live. Let them win.

Behind her, Tommy and Danny, her stalwart warriors, hesitated only for a heartbeat before continuing to flee in the opposite direction, the horror of the scene propelling them toward survival.

The rebels scattered, each to their own fate, but not before the hacktivists of the darknet, with hands trembling and hearts heavy, captured the moment on video as it streamed through Washington, D.C.'s surveillance system. They could hardly believe they were broadcasting a martyrdom in real-time — the self-immolation of a woman who had been their beacon, their leader, in the darkest hours of their existence.

And then ... Pilatus emerged.

He stepped from the cathedral's shadow as if he belonged in the sun. Tall, powerful, and untouchable, Pilatus's black hair gleamed under the light that should have destroyed him. But the sun bent to his will.

He was sacrosanct.

Without haste, Pilatus approached Sage's burning body with a predator's grace, his expression one of reverence — almost ... affection. His robes slipped from his shoulders, baring himself naked to the sun's rays, and he covered her with them, smothering the flames that consumed her with an effortless grace that belied the gravity of his actions.

With a tenderness they didn't know that his kind could express, the hacktivists watched as he cradled Sage's charred body against him.

"Not yet," he murmured softly, his voice barely audible, yet it echoed like thunder.

His fangs pierced his wrist.

Pilatus pressed the bleeding wound to Sage's blackened lips, forcing his ancient blood into her burned and broken body.

The transformation was instantaneous.

Her charred flesh knitted itself back together, raw and flawless. Her eyes, boiled away in agony, regrew, their luminous green now tainted with something darker. Her hair, once gone, cascaded back down her shoulders in silky auburn waves.

The watching rebels of the darknet could only stare in abject horror, helpless, as Sage's destroyed flesh knitted itself whole under the potent influence of Pilatus's blood, despite the sun's rays shining down upon them.

The transformation was nothing short of miraculous — or monstrous, depending on the eyes that bore witness.

With a possessive grip on Sage that spoke volumes of his intent, Pilatus turned to the CCTV camera.

His lips stained with his own blood, his fangs gleaming dangerously, he smiled.

He beamed with pride, as if he were a stage actor taking his accolades after a successful encore performance.

To the world, it was a promise of the horror yet to come.

Without a word, he scooped Sage's unconscious but healed body into his arms and disappeared into the shadows of the cathedral, leaving the world shattered.

The revelation sent a wave of dread through the rebels' ranks, leaving them to question the nature of the enemy they thought they knew. The implications were terrifying: Pilatus was more than a simple vampire tyrant to overthrow ... he was a deity to be feared, a force that bent the very rules they believed immutable.

And Sage, their leader, their heart, their savior, was now inextricably bound to him.

Tommy and Danny, along with the remnants of their group, huddled in the shadows of a derelict warehouse on the edge of the city that served as their makeshift hideout and a hiding place for their vehicles.

"What the fuck?" Danny said, as his cell phone buzzed. "It's from Fang-hater."

He opened the link the hacker had sent to him.

Tommy and Danny crouched in the dilapidated warehouse surrounded by their team, their bodies hunched over the cracked screen of Danny's phone. The grainy footage replayed on a loop, capturing their mother's burning body, her agonizing sacrifice ... and her unholy resurrection through Pilatus' blood.

They didn't breathe. Couldn't. The world narrowed to the image of their mother, engulfed in fire, arms outstretched in some silent plea to the heavens as her skin blackened and peeled away in sheets. The sun devoured her. Smoke rose like incense from her flesh, and still she stood — trembling, defiant, burning alive.

And then he stepped into the light.

Pilatus.

A god in wolf's skin.

He walked through the sunlight like it was his birthright — tall, sculpted, and untouched by the inferno that had nearly claimed her. He stripped the dark robes from his body and cast them over Sage's collapsing frame. The flames hissed as they were choked beneath the weight of his garment, a smothered scream of fire.

The brothers stared, paralyzed.

Pilatus dropped to one knee beside her. They saw him bare his fangs — not in malice, but in something far more obscene.

Reverence. Lust. Obsession.

He bit into his own wrist, and blood welled up, thick and bright as rubies. He pressed it to Sage's lips like a communion.

And forced her to drink.

Tommy flinched. Danny swore under his breath.

Time stretched, warped, buckled.

They watched in frozen disbelief as the wounds along their mother's body — gaping burns, ruptured blisters, scorched muscle — closed. Her skin re-knit, cell by cell. Hair sprouted anew from her skull in shining auburn waves. The corpse they had mourned seconds before twisted back into the woman they had known... but changed.

Tainted.

Resurrected by the monster they were sworn to kill.

Screams of rage ripped from Danny's throat to echo throughout the derelict warehouse. "I am going to fucking kill that bastard blood-sucker!" He continued to watch as the video started once more, and his hands trembled as they clenched the device tighter.

"Shut it off," Tommy ordered, his voice devoid of emotion, but the tremor in his hands betrayed the storm raging beneath.

But Danny couldn't move. His eyes were locked on the moment Pilatus smiled at the camera, as if he knew they were watching.

"He took her," Danny murmured, his voice hollow. "He fucking took her."

Tommy's jaw clenched, his knuckles whitening as his fists curled at his sides. But his face was stone.

"I am going to kill him!" Danny said, sprinting for the exit.

Tommy ran after him and stopped him, gripping his shoulder hard before demanding, "Stop! Mom wouldn't want that."

Danny jerked away to look at his brother in outrage, yelling, "Like hell she wouldn't!"

Tommy replied emotionlessly, "No, she sacrificed herself to make sure that we would live. If you go back now, your dead!" Then he turned away and walked to the vehicles, saying over his shoulder. "Besides, if anything, she would want us to kill her first."

Danny's head snapped up, his eyes wide with fury and disbelief. "What the fuck did you just say?"

Danny's chest heaved, his eyes filled with rage, but deep down ... he knew.

"We'll get her back," he said to his brother, his voice a fragile promise to himself.

Tommy's gaze was distant, cold. "No," he said, his tone devoid of hope. "We'll end her suffering."

The words hung heavy between them.

When the time came ... one of them would have to kill her.

And both of them knew it.

As Tommy got into the truck, Danny looked back in the cathedral's direction. Grief reflected upon his youthful face, as he thought, *He's right. Mom would want us to kill her first.*

EPILOGUE

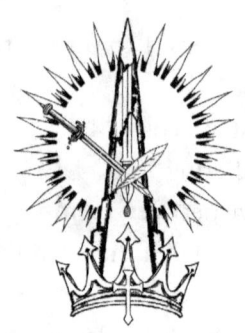

ECHOES OF DEFIANCE

A HUSHED MURMUR STIRRED the stale air as dawn's tentative fingers brushed the tops of the Blue Ridge Mountains. The rebels — my sons among them — had gathered in the dimness of our hidden base, a place I'd never step foot in again. I watched through the digital eye they didn't know I had access to, my heart aching with a bittersweet poison of pride and despair.

"Play it again," Tommy said, low and strained, like someone trying to breathe through grief.

He sat at the metal table in the command center as the room fell silent.

On the large screen, my last public moments replayed — my choice to face Pilatus, to expose his lies, to set the truth aflame even as my body burned with it. The screams. The light. The moment I gave everything to save them ... to show the world what monsters we were ... to save my sons ... even if it cost me everything.

My breath hitched at the memory. The echo of my heartbeat still throbbed in my ears.

"Look at her," I heard Danny whisper, his voice cracking. "She knew what it meant ... and she did it anyway."

My breath caught. I swallowed. The stone walls of my cell seemed to press closer, the cost of my choice wrapping around my ribs like iron bands and sat heavy on my chest, like the earth had already claimed me. They didn't need a martyr. They needed a mother. A leader. But all I could give them was a spark in the darkness.

A spark to ignite their revolution.

"Mom ... she ..." Danny couldn't finish, his voice trailing off into the silence that enveloped them ... enveloped me.

"Is there even a war left to fight?" Cherry's voice broke the silence, sharp and bitter. "We thought we understood the enemy. Sunlight doesn't kill them. They've been lying about that, too." Her eyes were twin pools of loss and anger.

"Sunlight kills some of them." Danny responded.

"But not the ones we need it to kill." Cherry stated. "Not the ones in charge. Not Pilatus!"

"Understanding changes nothing about our cause," Tommy replied, his tone as firm as it was hollow. He watched as his brother stood and paced the confines of the room, each step a measured beat in the silence that followed, before continuing. "We adapt, we evolve. Just like they do."

"You say that, but what if she's changed? What if she's on their side now?" Cherry whispered, her gaze fixed on the frozen image of Sage.

"She taught us everything we know," Danny cut in, pacing. "She *was* the rebellion."

"She was the deadliest warrior we had. Hell, she taught us all! What if ... What if we have to face her across the battlefield?" Cherry whispered.

"Then we do what must be done." Tommy's expression didn't change. His voice did — it dropped into something darker. "For the rebellion, for humanity. Even if it means..."

"Killing our own mother," Danny finished.

Tommy rose, pushing his chair back with a scraping sound that sliced through the gloom. He stood at the center of their pain, their purpose; casting a long silhouette in the flickering light.

"What my mother did wasn't about dying for the cause," he said. "It was about *living* for it. About making us believe in something bigger than survival. Now it's our job to carry the fire." His green eyes, so like mine, blazed with an inner fire. "She lit the way for us — for all those out there who can now see the truth."

On the screen, my burning body flickered into static. But in that static, fresh voices rose across the world — whispers in cathedrals, in alleys, in resistance bunkers. Vampires and humans alike passed my story like a torch in the dark. Images flashed in my mind's eye, scenes of a world beyond these four walls: humans and vampires alike, united by the story of a woman who dared defy an empire.

They didn't know me, but they carried my resolve, my hope, as their banner.

"Across the dark web, messages are pouring in. Stories of defiance, of courage sparked by Sage's sacrifice. She's ignited something far bigger than any of us could have hoped for," Tommy continued, conviction lending strength to his voice.

"She's being called a prophet in Madrid," said one rebel.

"A martyr in Johannesburg," said another.

The air felt thick with anticipation, the energy of the room shifting towards something new, something potent. Their faces revealed loss, but also a growing sense of purpose.

"Her name is being whispered in every corner where the empire casts its shadow," Tommy said. "She's become *the cause.*" His words were heavy with conviction, each one a weight that anchored their determination and gave it strength. "Our fight has only just begun."

I closed my eyes, letting my son's words wash over me. I leaned back in my cell, staring at nothing. I could almost smell the air outside, taste the mountain wind on my tongue, feel the solidarity of those gathered in my name.

For them, I was a beacon.

But here, in the darkness, I was still Sage Steel.

Still a mother. Still a captive. Still a monster.

Still the ember of a cause that would burn everything false to ash.

Across the globe, rebellion flared like brushfire; a patchwork quilt of resistance stitched together by shared outrage and newfound courage.

In the winding alleys of Paris, whispers echoed off cobblestone streets as humans passed clandestine leaflets, their determined eyes alight with a radical glow. High above the cityscape, a renegade vampire perched atop the gutted Cathedral of Notre Dame, casting a glance at the horizon — the promise of dawn no longer a harbinger of death but a call to arms.

In the sprawling metropolis of Tokyo, where buzzing neon lights battled with the darkness, a huddle of insurgents gathered in an underground bunker. A human hand clasped that of a vampire's. Former predator and prey united by common cause, their silent nod signaling the start of sabotage against the empire's oppressive machinations.

Half a world away, the dusty plains of Africa Sahel bore witness to
a lone figure standing defiantly atop a rocky outcrop. With eyes that
had seen centuries and a heart ignited with the fires of rebellion, a
vampire chieftain with silver dreadlocks called his clan to war against
their makers, urging them to break the chains Pilatus had forged
from fear and servitude.

Each act — each whisper of truth, each flare of violence — was a
ripple expanding across the ocean of subjugation the Crimson Empire had so meticulously cultivated. The mighty emperor Pilatus,
with his cold blue eyes and calculated grace, could sense the ground
quivering beneath his feet, a palpable unease that threatened to crack
and crumble his meticulously constructed empire.

Each rebellious act was a fissure in the facade, a warning of the
coming collapse.

And he *felt* them.

Like distant thunder before the storm.

I leaned against the door of my cell, my head turned toward the
opening in the door, out of sight of the camera in the corner almost
above my head. Even though I realized I was a monster, even I
had to admit that these ever-increasing vampire powers were kind
of awesome. My senses were on fire, the synopses in my brain were
firing faster than they had ever fired before.

It felt as though I could extract knowledge straight from the mol-
ecules in the air.

My new senses buzzed with violent clarity. I could smell every
drop of blood in the corridor. Hear every heartbeat in the wall.

So many things made sense now.

I couldn't see him, but I could smell him clearly.

He was behind me on the other side of this stone hall. Watching. Waiting.

I could hear his heart beat.

"I suppose you believe I owe you for making yourself scarce when my children came to rescue me." I breathed.

A beat of silence.

My voice would have been too low for a human to detect, but I knew he heard me.

His own reply was just as soft, "Not at all, my lady."

I chuckled briefly, then returned to my previous volume. "My lady. How ... quaint? What a strange way to greet me, Victor, or would you prefer I call you — Longinus?" I asked.

The words escaped my lips before I knew the truth. That name — Longinus — echoed from a corner of my mind that did not feel like mine. As if the blood in my veins now carried not just power, but memory.

Memory not my own.

Yes, it was like I knew so many things now.

Upon my words, I felt him tremble through the wall between us. It actually rippled through the stone.

"No." He whispered, like the name hurt his bones; almost as if the name caused immense pain or extreme shame, and even with my enhanced physical gifts, I almost didn't hear his reply.

"Then how about ..." I smiled, my whisper like ice, "Fang-hater?"

"As you wish ... Wraith ..."

The rebels' meeting neared its end when a soft ping pierced the hush, inconspicuous yet slicing through the tension like a knife. Heads turned toward the source of the sound: an old, battered computer sitting on a makeshift table, its screen flashing with the urgency of an incoming transmission.

"Is that ...?" Tommy began, hope threaded his voice as he moved in the machine's direction.

It had been two-weeks since they had seen their mother burn and since then they hadn't heard a word from her friend.

"Only one way to find out," Danny responded, beating his brother to the computer. His fingers flew across the keyboard, decrypting the coded message with practiced ease. "It looks like it's from Fang-hater ... and I think from mom!"

The rebels huddled close, their collective breaths held in suspense.

Lines of text bloomed across the screen, a mosaic of letters and numbers piecing together into coherent sentences. As the true meaning emerged, their expressions shifted from confusion to disbelief, then to cautious optimism.

"She's our ally ... inside the empire?" one rebel whispered, voicing the incredulity that gripped them all.

"Maybe," Tommy said, his gaze scanning the screen. "Maybe she's learned something ... something vital about Pilatus's strength."

To the Resistance:

You now realize that sunlight is no longer the salvation we thought it to be. It is a mirror — and in its light, the monsters wear familiar faces. But not all is lost. Few bloodsuckers can withstand sunlight. Only the first generation, and those they have directly shared their blood with, are completely immune.

Still, later generation vampires can attain this ability, though it is temporary. Their immunity is not divine. Or stolen from Christ. It's engineered. And we, the prey, have always been the key.

Understand this crucial truth about our adversaries. In order to bask in the harsh glare of the sun, to wield their uncanny strength and speed, they are bound by a singular need — melatonin.

Yes, the same hormone that grants us rest. It shields them. Strengthens them.

It's like an elixir for them, a potion that keeps their monstrous bodies from igniting under the sun's unforgiving rays.

Without it, they burn immediately.

Like I did.

The fanged monsters we fight don't need us. Not to live. Only to rule.

They don't need human blood. They just *want* it.

They can extract the precious hormone from any creature that roams this earth.

But they don't.

Because to drink from us ... is to dominate us.

To remind us that to them, we are livestock.

They also understand they could avoid our wrath completely, steer clear of our courageous resistance fighters all together, if they chose to only feed on beasts instead of us.

With their immortality, all they would have to do would be to outlive us.

If we die, if we vanish, the next generation and every generation hereafter won't remember freedom ... Their lullabies will be obedience. Their bedtime stories — rewritten history. And no one will tell them they were ever free.

But right now, we, the Resistance — we remember. The Resistance is legion! We possess the strength not just in numbers, but also an indomitable spirit that no Blood Monarch can ever hope to extinguish.

Our willpower is our greatest weapon, sharper than any blade and stronger than any shield.

It is the one thing that will free us from the yoke of slavery and the whims of the empire.

You must starve them. Cut off their access to their melatonin sources. Make them weak again.

Force the confrontation into the daylight — on *our* terms.

You hold the line between liberty and eternal servitude.

Let your courage be the fiery light that guides humanity out from under the thumb of this unending darkness.

Stand tall. Stand defiant. The light is ours to reclaim.

~ *The Wraith*

The room fell silent.

"She's *inside*," whispered one rebel.

"Or she *thinks* she is," Cherry muttered. "This could be bait."

"Let's not get ahead of ourselves," cautioned Danny, though his own eyes blazed with hope. "We need to verify this first. Tread carefully."

The room thrummed with whispered questions, but the message's enigmatic nature left much to the imagination. It was a clue, a lifeline thrown into the depths of their despair, hinting at the possibility of turning the tide against their immortal enemy.

Tommy's gaze lingered on the ending line.

The light is ours to reclaim.

With the meeting adjourned, the group dispersed, each member lost in thought, pondering the implications of this mysterious missive. However, Tommy and Danny had one last moment to share - a peaceful contemplation as dawn drew near.

Something they had done ever since they had lost their mother.

They stepped outside their mountain refuge, side-by-side beneath the trees at the cliff's edge, gazing out over the fog-shrouded peaks that stretched before them. The dark sky painted itself in hues of pink and orange, heralding the new day with a serene beauty that belied the chaos and horror of their world.

"What if it's not from Mom?" Danny asked softly. "What if Cherry is right? What if it's a trick?"

Tommy shrugged. "We check out the accuracy of the information. If it is true, great; we can use it. But you know this doesn't change what we have to do in the end. She wouldn't want to exist like that."

"I know." Danny murmured before leaning against a tree, fists pressed to his forehead, breathing through the grief like it was poison in his lungs. "She looked right at the sun, Tommy. I know what she was trying to do. It doesn't make it any easier." Danny's eyes glistened. "She taught us how to live," he whispered. "How to fight. How to survive. And now we're supposed to kill her?"

Tommy didn't answer. He just stepped beside his brother, rested a hand on his back, and let the silence speak for both of them.

They both looked off in the distance, absorbed in their own thoughts. Together, they watched the sunrise stretch across the blood-soaked earth, knowing that before the war ended, it would claim what was left of their family — one way or another — and

Tommy and Danny steeled themselves for the unthinkable possibility.

To save this world, they would have to kill the one person who had taught them to fight for it.

And the worst part was — she'd want them to.

REBEL RECRUITMENT

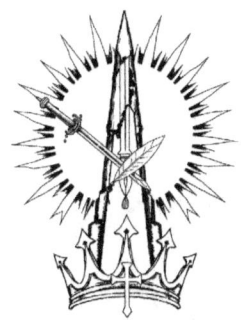

FINAL TRANSMISSION

YOU'VE HEARD THE TRUTH.
YOU'VE seen the empire's lies peeled back, layer by layer.
You've watched as monsters wore human skin ... and heroes became
something more.
And if you're still here, still breathing, still *feeling* —
Then you're one of us now.
The Resistance doesn't recruit by force.
It calls to those whose blood still remembers what freedom feels like.
To those who've lost everything — and choose to fight anyway.
If your heart shattered when she burned,
If your hands clenched when he smiled into the camera,
If the words of *The Wraith* lit something inside you that still hasn't
gone out —
Then listen closely.

They don't need us to survive.
They want us to kneel.
But we remember what it means to *stand*.
Cut off their elixir.
Burn their shadows.
Drag them into the light.
Because the truth is still ours.
And so is the fire.

We are the spark.
And this is how empires burn.

~ The Brothers Steel

THANK YOU FOR READING!

Did You Enjoy This Book?

Please tell your friends and don't forget to leave a review on Amazon and Goodreads!

Reviews and ratings like yours are the life's blood for independent writers and small publishers!

Want to see more by V. P. Nightshade?

Visit her Author Page on Amazon

https://www.amazon.com/author/vpnightshade

AUTHOR BIOGRAPHY

V. P. NIGHTSHADE

V. P. NIGHTSHADE'S LIFE in Texas is anything but ordinary; her grumpy old husband, two hormonal sons, an Alien Dog, a Cairn Terrier Princess who's extremely opinionated and talks, and new to the family in August 2023, a Cairn Terrier who Tangos! All this makes for an eclectic, and occasionally, chaotic family; and V. P. loves her family!

Readers can delve into the captivating world of paranormal romance with V. P., an author renowned for her spellbinding tales of forbidden love, ancient beings, and thrilling adventures. Let V.P. Nightshade's captivating stories immerse you in realms of danger and desire, where hearts are tested and souls are entwined. In her books you will discover a universe where romance blossoms amidst the shadows, where passion ignites beneath the moonlight, and where the lines between fantasy and reality blur.

If you enjoy the suspenseful twists, turns, or steaminess of authors like Sarah J. Maas, Stephenie Meyer, H.P. Mallory, Ruby Dixon, or Amber Foy, you'll fall in love with V. P. Nightshade's books!

Publishing costs are always increasing! Please don't wait; buy her novels now before the price changes!

Visit her Amazon Author page at:
https://www.amazon.com/author/vpnightshade
Visit her other Social Media:

https://linktr.ee/vpnightshade

www.ingramcontent.com/pod-product-compliance
Lightning Source LLC
Chambersburg PA
CBHW071914220626
47052CB00002B/347